THE
LOVE TRAP

THE
LOVE TRAP

•

Fran Shaff

AVALON BOOKS
NEW YORK

PRINTED IN THE UNITED STATES OF AMERICA
ON ACID-FREE PAPER
BY HADDON CRAFTSMEN, BLOOMSBURG, PENNSYLVANIA

For my sisters and friends who have been so supportive,
Elizabeth, Arlene, Colet, Dianna and Paula,
for my woodworker husband Jim,
for Mom, Dad, Zack and my cousin David.

Chapter One

Carly Ross leaned away from her drawing board and slapped her palms over her ears. "I can't stand that screeching sound one minute longer!" She walked to the front door of her antique house. Slipping into a pair of sandals, she tucked her pale yellow, peasant-like blouse into her full, gauzy, golden skirt.

Carly slammed the door behind her as she stepped onto the old floorboards of the front porch. "A woman can stand only so much noise while she is trying to work," she muttered, pounding down the steps. "It's indecent to expect your neighbors to listen to all those noises from the garage day after day." She crushed the springy grass with her enraged steps. "Do I make noise and bother him?" She was getting closer to the offensive garage. "He's an inconsiderate beast." Striding over the property line, she covered the last few feet to her new neighbor's garage.

The disabling, high-pitch sound that had driven her away from her work knifed the air again. Carly threw

1

her hands to her ears and entered enemy territory. "Turn that thing off!" she screamed, but her voice was no match for the shrill, offending cry of the machine.

The source of her suffering sat at a work table completely oblivious to her presence. His thick dark hair was speckled with sawdust and matted on the sides by the elastic of his safety glasses.

Carly folded her arms and tapped her foot. She waited several minutes before her preoccupied host noticed he was not alone.

He cut the machine and pulled his safety glasses off. "How long have you been standing there?"

"Long enough to lose my hearing," she replied through gritted teeth.

"What?"

Apparently he's already lost his, Carly thought, shaking her head. She opened her mouth to repeat her words but stopped short when she saw her neighbor pull something from each ear.

"Sorry," he said, smiling. "I forgot I was wearing these." He put the earplugs in a case on the work table. "Now, what did you say?"

Carly dropped her arms and strode a few steps farther into the garage. She stuck her hands into the pockets of her flowing skirt. "I'm Carly Ross. I live next door. You're making too much noise. You're going to have to stop what you're doing right now. I have work to do, and you are disturbing me."

He arched a brow and narrowed his ebony eyes. "*You* have work to do? What do you call this?" he asked, waving his hand over his workbench.

Carly threw her hand in his direction. "I call that disturbing the peace . . . neighborhood torture . . . a menace to society . . . and utter disregard for other people!"

He pushed himself back a few inches from his table. "And you're trespassing, Miss Ross."

"Trespassing!" Carly waved her fist toward the infuriating smirk that fueled her ire. "Why, I ought to . . ."

"You ought to what?" The smirk turned into an amused grin.

Carly took a deep breath. "Look, mister, I have six months of work to do in there," she said, pointing to her house, "and I have only four months to do it. I need to work. You're keeping me from it. You're costing me money."

"Are you going to sue me?"

His mocking tone set her on fire. "I'd love to."

"Well, in that case, you should know my name." He pushed himself farther away from the table.

Carly watched her neighbor move around the work bench and come toward her. She couldn't believe what she saw.

"I'm Devin Serrano. I go by Dev."

She stared at him, completely speechless.

"You don't need to examine it so closely, Miss Ross. It's a wheelchair just like any other wheelchair. It moves back and forth, side to side, even up and down a little."

His sarcasm was an antidote to her silent surprise. Carly folded her arms and leaned back on one foot. "Don't think for one minute, Mr. Serrano, that I'm going to back down just because you are in a . . . because you can't . . . because you're dis—"

"Because I'm a sit-down kind of guy?"

Carly pushed her hands back into her pockets. "You know what I mean. Standing or sitting, you're being inconsiderate of your neighbors, and I demand that you stop this instant."

He wheeled a little closer. He ran his eyes carefully over her from head to toe, then rested his gaze on hers. "As a matter of fact, I'm finished with the router today. I'm sure you won't be disturbed by it again."

Carly jutted her chin forward. "Fine. I'm glad we could reach an understanding." She spun around and started toward the door.

"Miss Ross."

She whirled around to face him. "Yes?"

"I can't guarantee you won't be disturbed tomorrow."

Carly spun back around to the door and bulldozed through it.

Dev watched her pound over his driveway onto his lawn. He wheeled to the edge of his garage and watched Carly crash angry steps all the way to her house. He leaned back in his chair and smiled. He drew in the deepest breath he'd drawn in nine months. For the first time since the accident, someone had treated him like a man instead of an invalid. He couldn't have been happier to meet Carly Ross.

Carly stomped up the steps of her porch with savage strides. "Words on deaf ears," she murmured through clenched teeth.

"Whose deaf ears?" a soft voice inquired.

Carly's eyes sprang to her right. "Malena." She softened her jaw. "I didn't see you sitting there."

Malena Sanchez rose from the wicker rocker and

approached her cousin. She folded her arms and grinned. "What are you so upset about?"

Carly shoved her hands into her pockets and tossed her head toward Dev's house. "My neighbor. He's working in his garage making too much noise. I can't get any work done."

"I don't hear anything."

"He said he's finished for the day, but he'll be back at it tomorrow." She yanked her hands from her pockets and dragged her fingers through her full blond locks. "I'm so mad I could spit enough iron and coal to make my own steel."

A chuckle tickled Malena's ribs. "All right, Miss Structural Engineer, let's not try to simplify the steel-making process too much. The point is that you are a little upset, and it's that new neighbor who's egged you on." She took Carly's arm. "Come on over here and sit down."

Carly followed Malena to the wicker loveseat next to the rocker. The two of them sank into the soft grass-colored cushions. Carly took a deep breath and forced a smile. "I'm sorry, Malena. I didn't mean to take my bad mood out on you."

"No problem. What are best friend cousins for?" She squirmed into a comfortable spot in the corner of the loveseat. "Now, tell me all you found out about this new man in town. I've seen him around. Looks pretty good to me."

Carly's eyes snapped to meet her cousin's. "Looks good? I suppose he does." She shook her head. "But he's a pain in the—"

"What man isn't?" Malena teased, cutting off her cousin and rolling her deep brown eyes. "The good news is they aren't always that way." She grinned and slid two fingers into the big, soft curls of her short molasses-colored hair. "And isn't it fun when they can be very, very agreeable?"

Carly laughed. Her twenty-four-year-old cousin had been keeping a watchful eye on the opposite sex since she was six. "Have you encountered any agreeable men lately?"

"I'm always looking for the perfect guy. You know that."

"Maybe you should introduce yourself to my neighbor. After all, you live only a few blocks away. It'd be very convenient for you to strike up a friendship with him." Carly shifted in her seat. "Maybe then he'd be too busy to bother me."

Malena brushed a finger over her tawny cheek and shook her head. "No, I've already checked him out. He's too old for me."

Carly's brows flew heavenward as she slid to the edge of her seat. "You checked him out?"

"Sure," Malena said, pushing her back deep into the soft cushion. "Hey, if a new guy moves into the neighborhood within six blocks of my house, he's under investigation. I'm not going to get a husband and a family sitting in my office all day with my nose glued to a computer screen."

Carly sank back into her comfortable seat. "I suppose not." She tilted her head. "So you're as determined as ever to be married by the time you're twenty-eight."

"Absolutely. I want lots of children so I've got to start young."

"Being the best computer programmer in Wisconsin

three years after getting your Master's degree isn't enough for you?"

Malena flipped the short curls at her neck. "Look, I know your career means everything to you, and that's perfectly fine. But my career comes second. I want a big, old-fashioned family. If I can fit my career around it, fine. Rapid success hasn't changed my mind one bit."

Carly nodded thoughtfully. She'd give her pinkie toes and two fingers to be one-tenth as successful in her career as her cousin. Being a top-notch structural engineer had been her dream since she was a teenager. Now her lifetime friend, three years her junior, possessed everything Carly had ever dreamed of, and it didn't matter to her one bit. She'd trade it all for a husband and children. Carly wished she had the goods to make an exchange with Malena instead of having to work so hard all the time. The genes were certainly distributed unevenly between them. Intelligence exuded from Malena even more than her breath-taking beauty and sparkling personality.

Malena waved a hand through Carly's field of vision. "Are you still with me?"

Carly smiled softly. "Sure."

"About your neighbor . . ."

"Yes?"

"He's too old for me, cousin, but thirty-two is the perfect age for you."

Carly sprang forward. "What?"

"Take it easy," Malena said, chuckling at Carly's stunned reaction. "I don't mean you have to marry the guy. All I mean is he shouldn't be that difficult for you to get along with. You know, talk with him and come to an understanding with him about what has upset you."

Carly sat back in her seat and swished her head from side to side. "I don't think so. Something tells me there won't be any reasoning with Dev Serrano."

Malena took a deep breath. "I'm not talking about logical reasoning with him, Carly. What I'm saying is he's a man and not bad-looking. You're a woman and pretty good-looking yourself. Why not try a little honey to catch this fly and coax him into quietness?"

Carly leaned forward and pressed her hand to her abdomen. Her stomach filled with knots at her cousin's suggestion. Was it because she wouldn't find another encounter with Devin Serrano appealing, or because she would?

"I know you'll do fine with him, Carly. You'll be neighborly and friendly instead of a nasty old grouch."

"But he's so infuriating—" *And sexy*, that little voice in her head added.

Malena extended her hand in front of her. "No excuses. You'll be neighborly whether you like it or not." Malena bounced to her feet. "Come on. Let's go inside. I need to go over a few things on that new program I was helping you with yesterday."

"Wait a minute," Carly said, grabbing Malena's arm. "Neighborly? What do you think I'm going to do? Bake a cake for him?"

"Or a pie," Malena suggested nonchalantly. "Men like both. Soften him up, and make yourself irresistible. Don't let him be able to say no when you ask him to be more considerate."

Carly raised a brow. "Do you think it will work?"

The screech of a table saw rang through the yard.

Malena glanced toward Dev's garage, then back at Carly. "You couldn't do any worse."

Quiet loomed over the neighborhood. Carly could no longer blame Dev for her lack of progress.

Or maybe she could. He hadn't left her mind since she saw him in his garage. The man sure could fill out a T-shirt. She didn't need to imagine what he might look like without it, either. She could see every well-honed muscle in his chest straining against the fabric.

Carly tossed a pencil at the drawing board and went to her computer. The clock in the lower right corner of the monitor told her midnight was only a memory now—a distant one at that. She yawned and stretched and decided she needed to get some rest.

She shut down her computer and went straight to the bathroom. Staring into the pooling water in the basin as she brushed her teeth, she swore she saw Devin Serrano's reflection looking back at her. She blinked her eyes and spit seafoam green toothpaste into the swirling water. She rinsed her mouth and resolved to stop thinking about her neighbor.

She slid into a pink cotton nightie and snuggled into the cool white sheets. *Malena was right*, she thought. *Dev is a handsome man, strong and confident*—She turned on her side and yanked the sheet over her head. *And completely infuriating.*

Carly pulled the sheet off her head and lay on her back staring up at the shadows on the ceiling. *He is a striking man.* She closed her eyes and told herself to go to sleep.

Ear-melting noise shocked Carly from her sleep. She bolted upright and rubbed her palms over her head. "He's at it already!" she said aloud, wiping sleep from her eyes and glancing at the clock. 10:00. It wasn't as early as she'd thought. Throwing back her covers, she got up, walked to the bathroom, and stepped into the shower. Hot water poured over her, washing the last of the sleep out of her.

Carly mentally rebuked the handsome Devin Serrano as she dried and dressed. The man was a problem she had to deal with, an irritation that had broken into her sleep, a distraction she had no time for. He was all that and every bit as handsome as Malena had said.

Carly shook her head. "Never mind how attractive he is," she said, scolding herself.

High-pitched noise screeched across the yard. Carly's irate approach hadn't worked. Maybe Malena's neighborliness idea would.

Carly went downstairs to the kitchen of the old two-story house. Her bare feet padded over the black-and-white tile. She opened the pantry and peered inside. No cake mixes. She'd have to make one from scratch.

A Betty Crocker cookbook leftover from the Johnson administration leaned against the side of the top shelf. Carly stood on tiptoe to reach it. She pulled it down and opened it up to the cake section, quickly finding a recipe suitable for her needs.

Carly started with margarine, then added sugar and eggs. As she measured the vanilla, a shriek louder than ever gashed the air between her and Dev's houses. She dropped a teaspoon of vanilla into the batter and stepped to the window over the white sink. She peered through the glass toward Dev's garage. "I wonder if I have any arsenic on hand," she queried aloud.

The noise subsided, and she went back to the mixer to complete her task.

By late afternoon the cake was cooled and frosted, and Carly had accomplished little at her computer or her drawing board, thanks to the distracting syncopated symphony of Craftsman tools pounding the windows of her home.

Carly lifted the coconut cake she'd placed on a sturdy paper plate and took a deep breath. "You'd better appreciate this, Devin Serrano." She took a few steps, then stopped. "Maybe I should have baked him a sweet potato pie. I could have called my little offering for peace the 'Silence of the Yams.'"

She scolded herself for being so feeble with her rare attempt at humor, then left to meet the enemy.

Chapter Two

Henry Williams sat on the sofa, making his line of vision even with Dev's. "Partner, you've got to do your exercises every day."

Dev straightened his spine and steeled his jaw. He carefully eyed his six-foot plus, dark-skinned physical therapist. "I won't be ordered around like a child. I'll recover at my own rate as I see fit."

Henry creased his forehead. "Don't you want to get back to the iron? Aren't you itching to be a part of putting up those big buildings again?"

Dev glanced around his living room, studying the dark maple flooring, the six-inch hardwood moldings, the out-of-place modern furniture, and the wide pathways for his wheelchair. He took a deep breath and rested his eyes on Henry. "I don't know."

"Didn't you like being an iron worker?"

Dev lifted an uncommitted shoulder. "It was okay, but a man's job isn't the only thing in his life."

A chuckle rumbled over Henry's ribs. "I'll say it isn't. I've got a wife and three kids to prove that."

Henry didn't look like the devoted family man he was. He looked like a hulk ready to pounce on the bad guys and put them in their places.

"Then you know what I mean, Henry. There's more to my life than iron and steel—even from the seat of this contraption." Dev wheeled himself to another spot in his living room. "I've been working on other things since I moved to Pine Grove. The physical therapy just isn't as important to me anymore."

Henry lifted a brow and twisted his mouth. "Other things, huh?" He glanced around the room, then back at Dev. "Like what?"

Dev shrugged and avoided Henry's eyes. "Other things. That's all."

Henry stood, tugged at the band of his jeans and turned to walk to the nine-paned glass at the end of the long, narrow living room. He placed a hand on the molding and looked out over Dev's yard, staring several long moments.

When Henry turned back to Dev he was wearing a grin the size of Texas. He nodded very deliberately. "I think I understand about other things," he said. He looked out the window again, then back at Dev. "Like something about five and a half feet tall, with long blond hair and a silky skirt flying out all around her?"

Dev leaned forward in his chair. "What?"

Henry glanced out the window one more time. "Looks like she's on her way over right now, and she's carrying a cake."

Since Henry was looking in the direction of Carly Ross' house, he had to be referring to her. If she was bringing him a cake, she'd probably poisoned it. "I'm afraid you're way off base, Henry. My neighbor would like nothing more than to see the moving truck back in my driveway returning me to Milwaukee."

Henry leaned a massive shoulder against the wall and eyed Dev carefully. "You sure?" He looked out the window again. "Doesn't seem like anyone's forcing her to come over."

Not directly, maybe, but Dev had worked in his garage all morning and part of the afternoon making as much racket as he could, hoping the noise would bring Carly back to his house again. He never thought it would be with a cake, though. An ax, maybe, or a gun, but certainly not a cake.

Her raging eyes had been like a storm at sea when she'd come by yesterday. Dev had thought of little else but those wild eyes that had ignited him with their passion. "Trust me, Henry, I'm sure. Carly Ross would love to see me vacate the premises permanently."

Henry shrugged and brushed a piece of lint from his orange T-shirt. "If it isn't a woman, then what's keeping you from doing your physical therapy?"

Dev wheeled toward the window and watched Carly as she came nearer. She *was* carrying a cake. He shifted his gaze up to Henry. "It looks like I'm going to have company, you merciless mercenary, so if you don't mind, I'll see you next week."

Henry pushed off from the wall and sent another grin at his patient. "You seem mighty anxious to see a woman who you say can't stand the sight of you." He craned his neck to catch one more glimpse of Carly. "And she seems a little too friendly bringing a cake to a man she'd like to get rid of."

"Door's right over there, Henry," Dev said, pointing.

"I'm going, but, Dev, if you won't do your therapy for yourself, maybe you should do it for that new little lady in your life." He took a deep breath, squeezing his chest tight inside its cotton binding. "Be real nice to stand and take her in your arms, wouldn't it?"

Dev's gut burned. Carly's provocative eyes weren't the only thing Dev had been dreaming about since he'd seen her. He'd been wanting to do exactly what Henry suggested—take Carly in his arms and see what it felt like to hold a hurricane against his heart. Dev looked away from Henry and wheeled to the front door. "With this one, if I tried anything like that, she'd put me right back in the chair. I told you she doesn't like me."

Delicate fingers rapped on the door.

Henry lowered his voice to a whisper. "Whatever you say, partner, but think about what I said. Whether it's the knockout on your front porch or some other woman, don't you want to be able to walk down the aisle some day?"

Dev's laugh burst from the deepest recesses of his body. "Marriage? Me?" He shook his head and slapped Henry on the arm. "That's for housebroken guys like you, Henry, not for men who enjoy their freedom as much as I do." Dev wheeled to the door.

Carly knocked again, a little louder this time.

"See you, Henry," Dev said, placing his hand on the doorknob. He opened the door. "Hello, Miss Ross. What a nice surprise. Come in."

Henry waited for Carly to enter. He greeted her, then gave Devin a stern look. "I'll see you next week, partner. I hope things will be going a lot more smoothly by then."

"One can always hope," Dev said sarcastically. He nodded at Henry and closed the door as the physical therapist descended his stairs. Turning to Carly, he said, "What brings you to my humble home, Miss Ross?"

Carly cleared her throat and tilted her head. She gave him a smile that a blind man could tell was insincere. "I made a cake for you . . . to welcome you to the neighborhood." She shifted her weight from one foot to the other. "I know I'm a little slow about the welcome, with you moving in a few weeks ago. I'm sorry I didn't come by sooner."

"But you did come over sooner, Miss Ross. Have you already forgotten yesterday's visit?" Dev asked, trying to limit the size of the smirk on his face.

Carly's cheeks reddened. "About that. I'm sorry if I came off as such an old crab. I'm usually not so grouchy."

"Grouchy?" Dev repeated, lifting his brows. "We Italians consider expressive temperament to be a sign of great passion. You had a point to make, and you made it."

The color drained from her face, and Dev panicked for a moment that she might faint right where she stood. He reached toward her. "So that cake is for me?"

Carly gave him a crooked nod and handed him the cake. "I hope you like coconut."

Dev set the cake on the coffee table ahead of the sofa. "I don't mind it," he said nonchalantly. "Won't you sit down?"

Carly followed the hand Dev pointed in the direction of the sofa and sat.

If she tried to hide the iron she held in her jaw, Dev didn't notice. She was obviously very uncomfortable and apparently still upset with him. Though she spoke calmly, the storm that had raged in her eyes the day before was still evident.

"I thought of making you a sweet potato pie . . ." she said, her voice trailing off.

She looked away. "Is that a Redlin print?" she asked, pointing to the framed art over the wood-burning fireplace.

Dev replied without looking at the painting. "Yes, Autumn Evening. The old brown clapboard house in it reminds me of this one."

Carly stood and walked to the print.

Dev followed behind her.

She reached toward the picture and took a deep breath. "I can smell the leaves burning," she said, as a smile of appreciation inched across her face. "I can tell the air is full of autumn crispness, and I can hear the children chattering about their days and their lives." Carly touched a fingertip to her lip. "Raking leaves as dark settles over a great big yard. I've done it many times."

Dev was touched by her reaction to one of his favorite works and by the sentimentality in her voice. "You like art, Miss Ross?"

She whirled and lowered her glance to him. "I suppose," she replied, lifting a shoulder. "I've never made a point of studying it, although I've seen some of Terry Redlin's work." She looked back at the print, then at Dev again. "I know what I like." She pointed a thumb over her shoulder. "And I like Autumn Evening."

Carly tugged at the round neckline of her gauzy blouse, then put her hands into the pockets of her flowing skirt and looked away from him.

Dev started to feel guilty that he hadn't done one thing to put her at ease since she arrived. She'd obviously come with a peace offering to make up for her wild outburst of the day before. The least he could do was let her off the hook. "Won't you sit down, Miss Ross," he said, extending his hand toward the sofa.

Carly walked back to the black vinyl couch and seated herself where she'd been before.

Dev wheeled next to the sofa. He pulled himself from his chair and plopped down next to Carly.

She drew in a quick breath as her fingers flew to her neckline once more.

He'd made her uneasy again with his sudden move to the seat next to her. The nervous twist of her blouse and the deep color of her eyes revealed her anxiety quite clearly. "Do you like music, Miss Ross?"

She gave him a crooked nod as she continued to curl the gauzy fabric of her blouse in her fingers.

Dev reached for a remote control and started the stereo. Vivaldi's Four Seasons began to play, and he saw her relax immediately. "That's better," he said, giving her a half-smile.

Carly released the nervous grasp on her shirt. She returned Dev's smile with a forced one of her own.

"You have an office at home?"

She bobbed her head up and down.

"What kind of work do you do?"

"I'm a structural engineer."

"Interesting," Dev said, stroking his fingers over his jaw. "There's something we have in common."

Carly sat forward, eyebrows raised. "We do? You're an engineer too?"

His laugh sounded more like a reaction to a punch line than one of civil amusement. "No, I'm on the working end of putting up a building. I'm an iron worker—or at least I was an iron worker."

A furrow grew in Carly's forehead. "Are you saying you don't think an engineer's work is real work?"

He lifted a shoulder. "In the sense that you get paid for your time I guess it's work. But you do it all sitting on your backside. Real work is done with your hands and arms and le—" He quickly averted his eyes.

Carly cleared her throat. She leaned back and twisted the neckline of her blouse again. "Is that how you got hurt? On the job?"

Dev glanced at the conveyance next to his sofa, then looked at Carly. He shook his head. He drew in a deep breath and slowly released it. "No, I didn't get hurt on the job. I was involved in a car accident. I was helping a woman with a flat tire when another car came by and hit me."

Carly sat forward and touched his hand gently. "Mr. Serrano, I'm sorry."

Reflexively, he sandwiched her silky fingers between his hands. He looked deep into her eyes a moment, then broke their connection by pulling his hands away. "It's no big deal. I'm fine." He reached for his wheelchair and pulled himself into it. "How about some coffee to go with that cake?"

Carly stood and walked around the low table. "I

guess so," she said, waiting for him to lead the way to the kitchen.

Dev picked up the cake and put it on his lap, then wheeled out of the living room and into the kitchen. He set the cake on the counter.

Carly leaned against the refrigerator and folded her arms. "Did he stop to help, the man who hit you?"

"They tell me he did. I was knocked unconscious on impact." He reached into a cabinet and pulled out two chipped china dessert plates. "The poor guy."

"Poor guy? The man who hit you? Why do you feel bad for him? Did he get hurt too?"

Dev rested his elbows on his chair and tilted his head. "Not physically, but in some ways he was hurt worse than I was. You see, he was on his way home from the hospital. His wife had just delivered a baby. He'd stopped by a bar with his brother-in-law and split a beer with him in celebration. Half a beer. That's all he had, but the cop at the scene of the accident smelled it on his breath and arrested him for DUI. Everything got real complicated from there, even though a blood test showed his alcohol level was well below the legal limit."

"What happened?"

"Once I was well enough, I testified for him. I couldn't stand to see a man's life ruined over a silly accident that was as much my fault as it was his— maybe more. I should have pushed the woman's car farther off the road, but it was dark and windy and raining buckets. I just wanted to get the job done."

Carly stared at him as though she didn't believe him. "You testified for him? You didn't sue him for a big settlement or anything?"

Dev grinned at her and leaned back in his chair. "Now what would I need a big settlement for? I can take care of myself. Always have, always will. The only settlement I took was for the medical bills. Our insurance companies worked that out."

Her eyes fastened themselves to his, and Dev looked as deeply into them as he could from six feet away. She didn't say anything. She didn't move. She just stared.

Carly Ross was definitely one beautiful woman. Long, full blond hair, voluptuous lips, rosy cheeks, delicate, slim fingers, a rounded figure that could drive a man mad. But it was her eyes that completely captivated him. The way she looked at him now, Dev felt as though her eyes alone could propel him out of his chair and across the room.

Carly abruptly raised her hands to her hair and pulled her fingers through the loose locks. "Could I help with the coffee?"

The unusual raspiness in her voice notched another mark in the column of sensuous things about her. Dev wiped a hand across the five o'clock shadow on his cheek and cleared his throat. "You can get a couple of mugs from the tree next to the fridge. I'll make the coffee."

Carly reached for the yellow mugs, one with a chip on the handle and the other with a worn blue flower on its front. A cup in each hand, she stepped to the sink and braced her hip against the edge.

Dev filled the pot with water and set it on the dark tan countertop. He pulled open a drawer and took out two spoons and two forks. He placed them on the dessert plates he'd taken from the lower cabinet. "Do you take milk or cream or sugar in your coffee?"

Carly set the mugs on the counter next to the dessert plates. "No," she said, brushing a crumb from the edge of the sink. She glanced directly at him. "I take it black."

Dev brusquely pulled himself from his wheelchair and stood. He braced himself against the counter with his left hand and took hold of the pot full of water with his right. Dumping the water into the reservoir of the coffee maker, he then reached into an upper cabinet and brought down the coffee and the filters. He settled them in the coffee maker and switched it on.

Still leaning against the counter, standing fully erect, Dev looked over at Carly. Her eyes were as wide as a freeway.

"I didn't know you could stand. I thought . . ."

"I've made some progress toward recovery," Dev said, gluing his eyes to the mesmerizing blue seas that, for the first time, rested below him.

"Oh," she said, forming her lips into a perfect circle. She started to twist the neckline of her blouse again, but she didn't say anything else. She just looked at him.

Dev moved a bit closer to her. He wanted to touch her, to cup her red-hot cheek with his cool hand. He wanted to watch her drop her lids and press her complexion deep into his palm.

Carly moved back a little and glanced around the kitchen, breaking the bond between their eyes. "Are you going to remodel in here?" she asked, a quiver in her voice.

Dev didn't take his eyes off her. He loved seeing

her from this higher perspective. She seemed so small standing next to him, so gentle and delicate. "Remodel? I guess it could use a good going over."

Carly's gaze drifted back to him. "Is that a yes?" she asked, coyly smiling up at him.

"Yes," he repeated. He could hardly stand being so close to her warmth, her fresh smell, her tempting shape without taking her in his arms as Henry had suggested. As he had dreamed the night before.

"The outside too?"

"Outside?"

Carly twisted over the sink to glance out the window. "I noticed your house needs painting. Are you going to change it or keep it like it is? The same color and trim, I mean." She looked back at him.

He lifted a lock of golden hair from her blouse and placed it behind her shoulder. "Just paint it. I like the color."

Carly took hold of the hair he'd touched and tucked her shoulder away from him. "It's easier that way, to just paint the same color. Especially a dark one, like brown." Her breaths were as shallow as her words.

A fly dove toward her nose, and Carly brushed it away. She blinked and focused back on Dev.

The fly made another descent. This time Dev moved to wave the little pest away. The jerky motion he made threw him off balance. He reached for the counter to steady himself.

Carly jumped as he started to fall and pushed backwards into the edge of the sink.

When Dev regained control of his body, his hands were gripping the molding on either side of the sink, and Carly was pinned between him and the porcelain.

Their eyes bolted together, and Dev instantly felt all the air leave his lungs.

Breathe, Dev reminded himself. In and out.

But breathing didn't come easily, not when he was this close to Carly. All he wanted was to touch her.

Carly's eyes turned a deep indigo color. The tip of her tongue slipped between her lips and slid from one corner of her mouth to the other. She looked as though she were going to speak, but she remained as silent as an empty room.

Dev couldn't move, and it wasn't his accident disabling him now. It was Carly Ross. She'd hit him harder than the car that had landed him in a hospital bed, and she hadn't laid a finger on him.

But she hadn't pushed him away either—not yet. Maybe she didn't want to push him away. Maybe she wanted him to touch her, kiss her. Maybe . . .

There was only one way to find out.

Chapter Three

The darkness of Dev's body loomed over her. His hair, the color of coal, the heavy, black beard contrasting with the whiteness of his skin, the dark T-shirt straining with each breath he dragged into his lungs. And his eyes, ebony circles that stole her very soul. She tried to pull free of his imprisoning gaze, but she was as helpless as a newborn kitten. Trapped between him and the sink, she was completely unable to move.

Carly blinked, hoping to break the spell, but when she focused on him once more his intensity was even more compelling.

He shifted his weight, moving his arms close enough to hers to tingle her skin with the soft, thick, jet-black hair on his forearms. She drew in a sudden breath and willed herself to push away from him.

But if she pushed him, he might fall.

His breath fanned her face, his eyes rained down sensual awareness, his scent coaxed her femininity to the surface, arousing womanly feelings she'd tucked away years before.

He moved closer.

She grew weaker.

Dev leaned lower. His lips lingered mere inches from hers.

She hadn't imagined he was so tall, so imposing, so totally enthralling.

Helplessness didn't suit her. She hated it. She had to do something, but she couldn't move.

At last she raised her hands to his chest in an attempt to urge him away before she did something she would most certainly regret. But touching him was a big mistake. The deep groan her kneading fingers drove from his chest undid her completely. The situation was hopeless. Nothing remained between them but surrender.

And Dev knew it too. Centimeter by centimeter, he edged closer.

Carly's breath nearly stopped in anticipation. Her eyelids fluttered then closed as she waited for the inevitable touch of his lips against hers.

With a crash, the sound of sharp claws assailed the kitchen door to the yard. Deep barks cut the air, then the sound of claws hit the wood again.

"My dog," Carly managed to say, her mind a world away.

Dev straightened up immediately. His eyes sprang to the door, then back to Carly. "Your dog?"

Carly squirmed her way out of Dev's entrapment. "He must have followed me over here."

Dev reached for his wheelchair and lowered himself in it.

Carly went to the back door and let her dog inside. She patted the golden coat of the small retriever and ordered him to sit.

"Nice dog," Dev said, wheeling toward the intruder. He stroked the top of his head. "What's his name?"

"Prints."

"Prince?" Dev placed a devilish grin on his face in an effort to cover his surging feelings. "I suppose his father's name was King."

Carly chuckled lightly. "No. His name isn't Prince like that, it's Prints as in blueprints. It's an engineering thing."

"Prints. I like it. He's been by to see me a few times since I arrived. Seems like a real nice dog."

Carly hugged Prints around the neck, then stood. "He is." She was grateful for the diversion, but a little disappointed. Was Dev?

"Does he like coconut cake and coffee?"

She smiled at Prints, then at Dev. "He'll eat or drink anything."

Dev waved his arm toward the table. "Then shall we?"

Carly went to the sink to wash her hands, then she took the two cups of coffee Dev had poured to the table.

Dev washed his hands, then cut generous pieces of cake and joined Carly at the gray and white Formica table. He placed their plates ahead of them and put Prints' cake on a piece of tin foil on the floor. Before he straightened up, the dog's cake was gone. "Healthy eater," Dev said, chuckling at the dog.

"I told you he'll eat anything."

Dev's eyes met hers. As he watched her, he tasted his cake. "Very good," he said, smiling.

She tasted her coffee. "Yours too," she countered, once again beginning to feel ill at ease with him.

Dev must have sensed her anxiety because he switched the topic to the weather and other mundane topics to take them comfortably through the consumption of their cake.

When they'd finished eating, Carly quickly made Prints' presence an excuse to leave.

"Thanks for bringing the cake," Dev said as Carly stood.

She walked to the back door. "No problem." She glanced through the milky view of the sheer curtain and out the window toward her house, then back at Dev. "I'd better get home."

Dev wheeled to the door and opened it for her. He patted Prints on the head. "Come back any time," he said. "Both of you."

Carly curtly bid him goodbye and bound down both steps at once with Prints. She sprinted across their yards without looking back. She needed to get home right away.

Her sandals sharply struck the steps as she made her way up to the front porch. She slid her key into the lock and let herself in the door, Prints swooshing in beside her. She closed the ancient walnut and leaned against it. "Whew! Home at last."

Carly stepped through the open foyer, past the coat closet and into the kitchen. She took a glass out of the cabinet, filled it with cool water and took a calming drink. She started to relax and her heartbeat returned to normal.

Then the screech of a table saw rang across the yard, and Carly's blood pressure shot back up.

She looked out the window above the sink and shook her head. "How could I be so dumb?" she shouted, smacking herself on the forehead.

Only she wasn't sure which stupid thing she'd done she was most angry about. Was it forgetting to talk to Dev about the noise reduction or for nearly letting him kiss her?

Letting him kiss her? She was practically begging him for it. She wanted him to kiss her—more than anything, she wanted to feel his lips on hers.

How could a man she wanted only to hate render her helpless with need for him? His noisy, selfish actions were stealing money out of her pocket by interfering with her work.

Carly grabbed a paper towel and stuck it under the cold running water. She wiped her face and neck with it, then braced herself against the kitchen counter.

If Prints hadn't come to her rescue—she couldn't think about what might have happened if her dog hadn't shown up.

"You foolish woman!" Carly said, scolding herself. "How could you behave so irrationally?"

There was no logical explanation for her behavior. Dev must have somehow beguiled her. That's what happened. He'd cast a spell on her, enslaved her somehow.

Carly glanced out the window over the sink once more.

He'd done nothing of the kind. She was merely a victim of sensual chemistry. The only thing Devin Serrano had done to her was to remind her of something she'd been trying to forget—that she was a desirable woman with desires of her own. But she had no time for fantasies. No one was going to launch her engineering business for her. She had to do it herself, and that would consume all the energy she could muster.

Carly tried unsuccessfully to work for the next couple of hours until she heard someone softly call her name from the front door. She leaned back in her chair. "Malena, hi," she yelled down. She rose and walked to meet her cousin.

"Am I interrupting?"

Carly took a deep breath, raising her shoulders high and glancing in the direction of Dev's house. "No," she said, looking back at her cousin. She inclined her head toward the source of the noise. "He is."

"This time I hear him. Did you go over and talk to him yet?"

Heat filled Carly's cheeks. She looked away from Malena and gestured at the sofa she was walking toward. "I went over today."

Malena joined her on the couch. "Did you take an offering of peace?"

"I baked a cake. From scratch. Coconut." Carly fingered her scalp and rolled her eyes. "I thought about baking a sweet potato pie . . ."

"No," Malena said, shaking her head. "Cake is better. Everyone likes cake. People like only certain kinds of pies."

"I guess."

"So what happened?"

Carly looked away. "Happened?"

"Yeah, what happened? I knew he wouldn't give up

his noisy activities all together, but did he at least agree to work only at certain times?"

"Not exactly," Carly said, trying to avoid Malena's gaze.

Malena frowned suspiciously. She twisted sideways and stared hard at her cousin. "Exactly what did happen?"

Carly lifted her shoulders and stood all in one motion. "Nothing, really." She walked to the large window that overlooked her backyard. A bed of tulips was in full bloom, red, white, yellow, and lavender. "We had cake and coffee."

Malena dogged her cousin's steps. She touched her shoulder and made her turn around. "It isn't like you to hold back on me, lady." She studied Carly's eyes until the sea-blue circles darted aside. "Noisy or not," Malena speculated with a grin, "I think you found your handsome new neighbor attractive, didn't you?"

Carly's eyes snapped back to Malena's. "Don't be ridiculous. We had cake and coffee, and I forgot to mention the noise. That's all. I'm upset with myself because now I don't have another excuse to go over and talk to him. I'll probably end up doing as I did the first time, attacking him in the garage. But that won't do any good." She rubbed her palms over her eyes, then drew her fingers through her hair. "I'll never get the Montgomery project started, let alone completed."

Malena took Carly's hand and pulled her back to the sofa. When they were both seated, she said, "Don't be so hopeless. He doesn't work all the time, does he?"

Carly shook her head and tossed her long locks over her shoulders. "I never heard him before last week."

"So chances are whatever project he's working on will be short-lived."

Carly tilted her head and wondered. "Maybe." Then another thought crossed her mind. "Or maybe he just waited until it got warm enough to work in the garage or maybe it took him until a few days ago to set up his shop. He's only been here a few weeks." She bounced off the couch. "You want some coffee?" she asked, walking toward the kitchen.

"You have some made?"

"I've got instant cappuccino."

"I drink that all the time."

Carly pulled mugs from the cabinet next to the stove and filled them with water. She put them in the microwave and set the timer. While she waited, she leaned against the counter and folded her arms.

Malena sat at the tiny drop-leaf maple table. "Did you get much accomplished today?"

Carly raised one shoulder and let it fall. "I had a few extremely lucid moments and got some quality work done, but I've got to get moving on that big Montgomery project. Right now I'm working on the little projects that are paying the bills so I can work on the big one."

The alarm rang on the microwave. Carly retrieved the cups of hot water and stirred in the cappuccino mix. Then she took the mugs to the table, handing one to Malena as she sat. She lifted her cup to her mouth and sipped carefully. She squinted at Malena. "Remember what we were talking about yesterday, you dating Devin Serrano?"

Malena tore her lips away from her mug and shook her head. "I told you he's too old for me."

"No, I mean when I said if you were seeing him, he'd be too busy to work in his garage so he wouldn't be able to bother me."

Malena took another sip of coffee. "I remember. What about it? I repeat, he's too old for me."

"I get it. Don't worry, I'm not thinking about trying to fix you up with him. I wouldn't do that to you." Carly grinned and cocked her head. She drew in a sip of coffee. "However, there isn't any reason why I can't run a few other young ladies in his direction. All I need is one for him to take an interest in. If I can get him started dating regularly, then at least my evenings would be quiet enough to concentrate."

"Interesting plan. It could work."

"Are you kidding?" Carly asked, pushing herself away from the table. She went to the window over the sink and looked at Dev's house. She turned back to Malena, leaning on the edge of the porcelain. "It's surefire. He's a great-looking guy, and I know plenty of attractive women. It's just a matter of finding the most compatible."

Malena leaned back in her chair and let a huge smile consume her face. "So you did notice how handsome he is." Her smile lingered and inched toward amusement. "I've never seen you like this before, Carly." She moved forward, placing her elbows on the table. "While you're looking for someone for him, could you keep your eye out for someone for me?"

"Maybe I will, but first I've got to concentrate on taking care of him. I'll make a profile of everything I know about him and compare it to all I know about the eligible women in town." Carly rubbed her hands together. She turned and leaned over the sink, staring out the window. "Poor Mister Devin Serrano won't know what hit him."

Malena popped up from her chair. "Well, it looks like you're on your way to solving one problem by creating another, so I'll leave you to your devices," she said, teasing her cousin. "What I came over for was to borrow a Phillips screwdriver. I can't find mine."

Carly pointed to her junk drawer. "I have one in there. Help yourself."

Malena took the tool. "Good luck with your little love trap, Carly. Just make sure you don't get caught in it yourself."

Carly scowled at Malena as she left. Sometimes her cousin said strange things.

Carly went to the built-in desk at the end of the cabinets in her U-shaped kitchen. She pulled out her address book and began to look over the names of her single acquaintances. She decided that before she could choose possible mates to link with Dev, she'd better list her neighbor's assets and interests. Then she'd list the interests and assets of her single lady friends, put them next to Dev's list, and choose his perfect match. She couldn't lose.

She wrote his name at the top of a notebook page in black ink, then she listed what she knew about him. *Dark hair, dark eyes, well over six feet tall, an utterly male scent that lingered even after he was gone . . .* She suddenly found herself waving a hand ahead of her face trying to cool her burning cheeks.

She ordered herself to put some distance between her clinical assessment of him and the extreme fascination she'd experienced earlier. This was business. She had to approach her tactics as she would in any business situation.

Iron worker, she wrote, *muscular build, wears a T-shirt like a sculpted statue, likes dogs, owns his own house, makes a good cup of coffee, likes woodworking so he must be handy in fixing things too, irresistible scent.*

Carly drew in an exasperated breath. "I already wrote about his aroma," she said, drawing a line through her last observation. She shook her head. Why couldn't she get the smell of him out of her nostrils? She'd never noticed such a thing about a man before, unless he'd bathed in aftershave. But Dev didn't smell like cologne.

Just what did he smell like? Carly tapped the pen against her brow and let her mind drift. He smelled like power and strength, virility and sensuality, potency and masculinity.

"Those aren't smells!"

She wrote again. *Likes art.* She scratched her head. Does he? She'd only noticed that one print above the fireplace. She shrugged and decided to leave that assessment in. *Muscular, hair-covered forearms, piercing eyes . . .*

She sat back and examined her list. "That's enough to go on," she said, satisfied. Then she looked through her address book again, hoping to find a match that would keep the man next door busy enough to give her all the peace and quiet she could ever want.

Some time later, two names had made the final cut—two attractive women of different shapes and sizes, each with a profession she could use as an excuse to get them together with Dev. Certainly one of them would distract him enough to make him turn off his tools.

"Carly," she told herself, "you're a genius." What had Malena called her plan? A love trap?

Carly smiled and agreed with her cousin's assessment. "A love trap . . . and I've got the perfect bait."

Chapter Four

Dev adjusted the light in his den and returned to his canvas. He stared at the painting he'd tried to work on all night long. He hadn't been able to expose her, not her inner self, the one he saw through the depth of indigo eyes. He'd never be able to paint an actual likeness of Carly, but ever since their encounter in his kitchen the day before, he knew he had to reveal in colors and textures the inside of her that had intrigued him to the point of madness. Yet, since he couldn't identify it or liken it to anything he'd ever experienced, he couldn't paint it.

Neither could he abandon it. He wanted to hold that part of her that had seized him so deeply. Obviously, he couldn't take her in his arms, but if he could paint her, he'd feel as though he had a part of her within his grasp. In some way he had to possess whatever it was about her that shook him down to his socks.

As dawn gave way to full sunlight, Dev rubbed his hands over his tired eyes. He yawned and stretched his bulging arms over his head. He needed sleep.

Dev wheeled his chair to the doorway of his den. Before he exited, he looked back on his blank canvas and the pile of crumpled drawing papers on the floor. He moved his eyes upward and let them drift over the den he'd turned into a studio. Paints, pencils, charcoals, pastels, sketch pads, canvases, easels, palettes, brushes, paint thinners, everything an artist needed filled that little room. Except guts.

He hated the room. He loved the room. It blessed him and cursed him at the same time. It manipulated him, distracted him, fascinated him, inspired him, and antagonized him. It was both his salvation and his greatest cross in life.

Iron workers aren't artists. Filling canvases with scenes or people or observations isn't a man's work. Sure, he was using his hands, but not in a virile way. Work that took power and strength like welding and bolting steel together forming the skeleton of a high-rise building, that was the work of a man.

Yet he couldn't keep himself from his studio. At first, when he could barely move and the pain seared his mind, his art supplies and the ability to tinker and create and explore an interest he'd always secretly held got him through the weeks immediately following his injury. But after those first weeks, his interest in art was no longer a clandestine curiosity. It became a passion, a drive so intense it was a part of him. He could no more ignore this urge to be an artist than he could ignore his need to breathe.

But iron workers aren't artists.

Was he an iron worker or an artist? As long as he remained in his wheelchair, he couldn't be an iron worker. He didn't have to make a choice.

Dev glanced around the den studio one more time, then wheeled out and closed the pocket door. He was too tired to choose. Besides, no choice was necessary today.

The day had been exceptionally quiet. Carly never heard so much as the sound of a window opening next door. She worked so intently on the Montgomery project that the day had passed away before she realized she'd missed lunch and dinner. She'd intended to work only a few hours on the big project and spend the rest of her time on the little ones that paid her bills.

No matter, though. She wasn't going to chastise herself for setting aside her little income earners when her speculative project had gone so well in the silence of the day.

As the sun lowered in the sky, Carly set her work aside. She went to the kitchen to get something to eat. She sat at the table with a ham sandwich, a bowl of salad, and a glass of milk. A small piece of paper with a name lay next to her plate. Carly touched two fingers to the paper. Meka Tanabe. She was the first woman Carly had chosen for Devin Serrano.

Meka was a gardener and yard worker. Dev was in desperate need of someone to care for his unruly yard. Not only was Meka advanced enough in her work to have authored a number of articles on the care of various yard-dwelling plants, she was a beautiful woman.

Like Dev, she had very dark hair and eyes. Her pale skin glowed. The striking beauty of her rounded face was magnified by healthy red cheeks and lips. She might be a little short for Dev at five feet one, but that would be up to him to decide.

Carly finished her dinner and took her dishes to the sink. She looked out the window and saw a light on in Dev's house.

The sun was disappearing. The day was almost over.

Carly rinsed her dishes and quickly decided she had to strike before the day was completely over.

She ran upstairs to her bedroom suite and tore out of her clothes. She showered and made herself presentable in jeans and a short-sleeved gold and blue plaid shirt. She slipped into some sneakers and left to find Dev.

It was dark out by the time she stepped onto her front porch. Crickets sang and a breeze filled with the sweetness of peonies drifted over the neighborhood. Carly leisurely descended the stairs in front of her house and walked the unmarked path to Dev's. She went to the front door and knocked.

No answer. She knocked a little louder. Still no answer. This time she pounded as though she were the narcotics police on a bust. Dev still did not respond.

Carly stepped to the window of his living room and peered inside. The house looked empty.

She released an exasperated breath. She'd really wanted to get her plan underway, but she decided there would be no harm in waiting another day.

She walked back down the porch steps. She traced her tracks over the sidewalk and driveway and onto Dev's side yard. A huge maple tree stood on the property line. In the brightness of the moon, the leaves shimmered a silvery green. Carly walked to the tree and raised a hand to touch the appealing texture. She pulled one of the leaves from the branch and touched it to her face.

The sound of a twig snapping came from behind her. She whirled around and stumbled, pressing her back into the massive trunk of the tree.

A dark figure overshadowed her and strong, piercing eyes bore down on her.

Reflexively she pressed her back tighter against the tree. Her heart pounded in her chest.

"Were you looking for me?" A deep, husky voice vibrated the thick air.

"Dev?" Carly inquired, barely able to speak.

Holding onto the overhead branch nearest to her, he brought himself closer. "Who else?"

She couldn't see his face against the slivers of moonlight that silhouetted him, but she could tell from the way he said his words that he was probably smiling at her with that mischievous grin she'd seen on him the day before. He seemed to delight in making her uncomfortable.

"What are you doing hiding in the shadows?" she asked resolutely.

"I wasn't hiding. I came outside to work my legs. The branches on this tree are low enough and close enough together that I can use them as braces while I walk and exercise my legs. And the tree is large enough to give me a good workout."

Her eyes dropped to his lower limbs. His thighs strained against the fabric of his jeans. It was difficult to imagine that such potent muscles were ineffective in supporting Dev's weight.

Slowly her eyes traveled upwards, surveying his body in the dark. In shadowy profile, his powerful frame appeared even more robust. With his hands grasping the branch above them for support, his biceps swelled into rounded, hard surfaces firm enough to crack walnuts on, but supple enough to entice a caress.

"I've never seen you out here before," she said, hoping her fascination with him didn't reveal itself in her shaky words.

"Probably not. The few times I've come out, I worked in the dark." His chest twitched as a chuckle rippled over his Adam's apple. "If I'm going to make a fool of myself and fall, I plan to do it in the dark. I don't need an audience."

"Have you ever done that?"

He turned his head enough to bathe his face in the moonlight, and Carly could see he was amused. "Made a fool of myself?"

Heat rose in her cheeks. "No, fallen."

He pulled himself up a bit higher and inched a little closer. He moved his face back into the shadows. "I just said I wouldn't want anyone to know that."

She looked down at the grass, then back up at him. "Sorry."

He moved a little closer. "I'm not," he said, lowering his voice.

He'd corralled her again. This time she was between his frame and the trunk of the tree. Remembering the vulnerability that had overcome her the last time she found herself in such a dangerous position, Carly knew she had to act fast.

She stepped away from the bark into an unconfining position. She had to move before he got any closer.

She didn't trust what he might do, or worse yet, what she might do. "You know," she started, trying to regain the composure undermined by his presence, "I noticed your yard is getting a little unkempt."

He straightened up and took another firm grasp on the branch above him. He scanned the surroundings in the moonlight. "Unkempt?" He looked back at her. "I noticed that too. I've got a riding lawnmower on order." He moved one hand to a branch nearer Carly, then moved the other and took two steps. "Is that what you came to see me about? Are you lodging a complaint about the way my property makes the rest of the neighborhood look?"

"No," she said, reaching toward him and touching his chest. "I didn't mean that at all."

He glanced down at her hand, then back at her.

Suddenly realizing she'd touched him, she pulled her hand away as though it had been burned. "What I meant to say is that I know a very good gardener. I thought you might want to hire her."

"Hire someone to do my yard work?" He glanced around again at his surroundings, then back at Carly. "I hadn't thought of it. I usually do my own."

"I used to too, but I found it took a lot of time I could otherwise spend working, so I started hiring someone." She wanted to be sure he got the right idea—that she was trying to help—whether it was true or not.

"And you've got someone whose work you're satisfied with?"

He was taking the bait. Carly nodded vigorously. "Meka Tanabe. She knows everything about yard care.

She's even written a number of articles about it. In fact, she's working on a book."

He moved again, and she could feel him fasten his eyes on her. "I don't put much stock in whether or not she can write about yard work. Doing it properly is all I care about."

She wasn't sure if he actually was getting closer again or if it just seemed that way. Carly took another step back. "Then you'd have nothing to worry about with Meka. She's the best."

One powerful hand moved to the next branch, then the other. "I hope you don't mind if I continue my workout while we talk. I try to make my way around this tree at least half a dozen times."

"No," Carly said, realizing at last that the reason he was advancing toward her was to continue his physical therapy.

Dev moved his right foot ahead, then the left. He was within inches of her again. "This Tanabe, she can handle a lawnmower, trimmer, hedge clippers?"

Carly took a step back as she nodded enthusiastically. "No problem."

He moved forward to the next branch. "She knows how to run a tiller and an edger?"

"Uh huh," she said, regressing again.

He continued ahead. "She can manage a spade, a hoe, a rake?"

Her retreat proceeded. "All those tools and more."

His onward progress persisted. "She understands the difference between weed killer and fertilizer?"

Carly stuck a leg behind her again and started to stumble.

Dev instantly reached an arm toward her and caught

her before she fell. Reflexively he pulled her against himself. "Are you all right?"

Pressed against him, his chest heaving into her side, she didn't feel at all okay. She answered with an automatic response. "I'm fine."

Moonlight caught his eyes. There was genuine concern in them. "You're sure?"

She didn't know how she managed a nod, but she did.

"Good," he said, letting her go. "Be careful. Don't trip over my chair again."

Carly looked behind her and realized she'd backed into his wheelchair. "I hope I didn't damage it."

Dev moved his hands to the next branch and took two steps. He reached for his chair and seated himself inside it. "If it can take the mishandlings of a big guy like me, I don't think you could hurt it that easily."

Carly laughed lightly and agreed.

"Would you like to come inside? I still have some of that coconut cake left, and I could make some fresh coffee."

Be alone again with Dev in that compelling kitchen? It was too risky. "Thanks, but I should get home."

The silver light caught his smile and showed a sweetness she never guessed she'd see in a man like Devin Serrano. For a brief moment, she almost changed her mind.

"Okay," Dev said, putting his hands on the guides of his wheels. He turned his chair in the direction of his house. "Thanks for the recommendation of the gardener."

Carly reached into her jeans pocket and pulled out a slip of paper. "Here's her number." She handed him the paper and took a step away. "I'm sure you'll like her. She's wonderful." She took another nervous step back.

Dev set his elbows on the arms of his chair. "I'll take your word for it."

Carly inclined her head toward him. "Good night." Abruptly, she turned and walked away.

Devin watched her glide through the moonlight like a swan floating on a lake. It was the first time he'd seen her legs. She'd always been wearing full skirts and gauzy blouses when he'd seen her before. Now, in jeans and a tucked-in shirt, her tiny waist and rounded hips were no longer hidden. Her long, shapely legs were exposed through the snug fit of the denim. Her figure was every bit as tempting as he'd imagined.

Carly walked up the steps of her porch and went inside her house without looking back. Dev smiled appreciatively at the determined way she carried herself. Carly Ross was definitely a woman who knew what she wanted and pursued it with vigor. As far as he'd been able to ascertain so far, what she wanted was to be a successful engineer. Nothing wrong with that.

Dev turned his chair toward her house. He looked up at the tree above him. Suddenly he stood and grabbed hold of one of the branches. His eyes moved to the trunk of the tree where Carly stood when he came up on her. Silver light had rained down on her, illuminating those spellbinding indigo eyes, and his heart was lost again at once. What was that power that made him need to understand what he saw inside her? He was grateful for the need to steady himself on the branches above. Had he been recovered enough to let go, he'd have taken her into his arms—and probably scared her away.

Perhaps if he'd held her, though, if he'd laced his fingers through her spun-gold hair and drawn in a breath at her neckline, he'd have begun to discover the secret her eyes had only tempted him to learn. And if he had kissed her . . . would her lips reveal the private knowledge he longed to discern?

Dev drew in a deep breath and stared towards Carly's house. He saw her figure through the sheer panel in the living room as she leaned over to extinguish the light that left him in the dark. Unable to see her any longer, he moved on to the next branch and the next, working his legs, until he came around once more to his chair.

He plopped down into the leather and started wheeling himself toward the house. Once inside, he decided he couldn't endure another night facing an empty canvas, no matter how much Carly had again roused his curiosity about the secrets of her soul. He needed sleep, not bewilderment. And he had to stop thinking so much about his neighbor. She was career through and through, and he had enough to deal with in his life already. He didn't need a woman complicating things for him even further.

He wheeled to the window at the end of the living room and looked one more time at Carly Ross's house. Then again, maybe she'd be worth a little complication.

Carly curled under the cold sheets and smiled with satisfaction. Step one accomplished. Dev would meet Meka in a few days, and she'd be spending lots of time with him. His yard needed work everywhere.

Being the gentleman he seemed to be, Dev would almost certainly ask Meka inside for some cooling refreshment. It would give the two of them the perfect opportunity to get to know each other. It was only a matter of time before Dev got used to having Meka around and started thinking of her in a social way instead of someone who worked for him.

Meka was a striking beauty. What man could resist her?

And what woman could resist Devin Serrano? He was six feet two inches of pure masculinity.

Carly took a deep breath and slid into a comfortable position. Things were going to work out just fine. Dev would be too busy with Meka to work in his garage, and Carly would have all the quiet she needed to complete her jobs.

Meka and Dev. As Carly imagined the two of them together, a knot formed under her ribs. Was she doing the right thing?

Chapter Five

Carly finished up two of her small jobs during the quiet time of the next few days. After she'd met with her clients to tie things up, they referred her to two new clients who had similar small projects. It was late morning when she returned home to begin work on her new assignments.

As she turned into the cracked concrete driveway that led to her garage, Carly noticed Meka Tanabe's pickup truck parked in Dev's driveway. She smiled as she pulled up next to her house and exited the car, pulling a portfolio and briefcase along with her. Her grin broadened as she traced the steps along the sidewalk and walked up to the porch. She paused there momentarily and stared toward Dev's property.

Now it starts. Meka and Dev. That annoying twinge she had felt before when she thought of Meka and Dev together tugged under her ribs. Carly twisted and rubbed her abdomen until the pain disappeared.

Then she saw him.

And he saw her.

As though she hadn't masterminded a sneaky plot to distract Dev, she waved and smiled at him.

The innocent lamb waved back.

Pushing down a feeling of guilt over the love trap she'd concocted, Carly moved toward her front door as casually as she could manage. She glanced toward Dev again just before she went inside.

He was still watching her.

She waved once more, then stepped inside. Within the security of her walls, Carly took a deep breath and let it out as she thought about her reaction to seeing Meka in her neighbor's yard. Why did she feel so guilty? All she'd done was recommend a gardener to Dev. She hadn't set him up on a blind date without his permission, even if it felt like she had. Whatever happened between Meka and Dev would be their own doing. If they happened to like each other and started spending lots of time together, Carly certainly wouldn't mind the quiet Dev's distraction would bring.

As she thought about Dev and Meka getting close, that annoying little knot tugged at her again. She massaged the pain under her ribs until it disappeared.

Carly looked out the window. Meka and Dev appeared to be discussing an overgrown bush. There was plenty of quiet to enjoy for the moment. Carly needed to take advantage of it. She went straight to her bedroom to change out of her business suit and into her favorite work clothes, a flowing skirt and peasant blouse. With quiet and comfort on her side, Carly eagerly settled into her work area and began to create.

Two hours of high productivity and blissful peace passed. From time to time Carly glanced out the window to see Dev and Meka working in the yard. Pleased with herself, she'd smile and return to her work, but that aggravating little knot under her ribs kept coming back every time she saw Meka and Dev together.

After a late lunch, Carly sat at her desk working on her computer. The sound of powered hedge clippers filled the air, and she shrugged it off. She was pretty sure she could tolerate a little noise without losing her train of thought.

The buzzing rolled over the air, louder, quieter, louder, quieter. Sustained high-pitch grinding, then low rumbling. Silence. More silence. Then a chainsaw, ten times louder than the clippers. A mower engine ripped the air, and Carly threw a pen at the computer monitor. "Has he got an entire army over there?"

Carly flew to the window and peered out. Dev was on top of a riding mower, moving it around the yard. Meka secured a chainsaw and sliced some of the dead hedges just above the roots. The idle clippers lay on the ground near the bushes, patiently waiting until Meka needed them again. Dev had a big yard. He'd be on that mower for a long time. Meka had a week's work left on the badly neglected hedges that surrounded the back and one side of Dev's yard.

"Great plan," Carly told herself. "This is even worse than before."

Carly glanced at the clock. She had some errands she'd been putting off. She decided to do them now. Dev would be done mowing by the time she got back.

When Carly returned with a few bags of supplies,

the neighborhood was once again peaceful. She quickly put her things away and went back to her computer. She'd barely begun when the roar of a gas-powered trimmer vibrated the air.

The front door swung open.

"Carly, you here?"

"In the living room, at the computer."

Malena came in carrying a bag of fruit and the screwdriver she'd borrowed. "Come on out to the kitchen and have something to eat. I got all your favorites."

Sometimes Carly wondered if Malena was psychic. She always seemed to know when her cousin was in dire need of her kindness. "Pears?" Carly asked.

Malena led her to the kitchen. "Yes, and mango and strawberries and bananas." She set the plastic grocery bag on the table and took out the fruit. She turned to a cabinet and took out a couple of bowls, placing the fruit inside them.

Carly sat at the table and reached for a napkin.

Malena washed the fruit, then set it on the table. She pointed to the screwdriver she'd laid near the empty bag. "Thanks for the use of the tool."

"Any time," Carly said, reaching for a pear. She took a bite and caught the juice on her chin with a napkin. "Mmm," she said, smiling. "This is perfect."

"Good. You can't be sure of pears in May. Who knows where they come from?" Malena took a pear and tasted it. She rolled her eyes and smiled. "Like you said, perfect."

"Aren't you home from work a little early?"

"Hey, it's Friday, and I've had enough for the week." Malena took another bite of pear. "Besides, I have to go fishing tomorrow. I promised a couple of people from the office."

"Have to? You love fishing."

"True," Malena said, wiping juice from her mouth, "but not with Ginny Michaels and Hector Winsted— especially Ginny Michaels. She's one of those people who go on and on about all kinds of boring details when she's telling a story. Sometimes, I wish her conversation would hang in the air so I could take a red pen and cross out all the useless words and get her to shorten up her stories."

Carly took another bite of pear and smiled. "Just because you're going fishing with them doesn't mean you have to be right next to them, unless you're renting a boat."

Malena thrust her hands out in front of her. "No boat! The quarters would be too close, and I'd end up jumping overboard to drown myself."

Pear juice started to go up Carly's nose when she laughed. "You always prefer shore fishing anyway."

Malena tilted her head as she took another bite and chewed. "I was thinking," she said slowly.

Carly recognized the plotting look in Malena's eyes. It usually meant she was up to something that Carly wouldn't like.

"You could use a little R and R. Why don't you come fishing with us?"

Carly nearly slammed her ribs into the table as she sprang forward. She stabbed a thumb to her chest. "Me?" She couldn't hold back a giant giggle. "You make the outing sound so tempting," she said sarcastically, "but you know I'd rather have my teeth drilled without novocaine than go fishing."

"Oh, come on, Carly. You need to get away from your work."

Carly finished her pear. "That's the last thing I need," she said, pushing away from the table. "I need to work night and day if I want a chance at that Montgomery project."

Malena set the remainder of her pear on a napkin and stood. She followed Carly to the sink. "A little fresh air would do you some good."

"Then I'll open the window." She turned on the water and washed the stickiness off her hands.

"It's always more fun with four people than three," Malena said.

Carly watched Meka trim the grass next to Dev's garage. Suddenly, her face brightened, and she swung around to face Malena. "You're right. Four people is more fun than three."

The shock on Malena's face mingled with a smile of anticipation. "You'll come?" She shook her head. "I never thought I'd see the day when you'd agree to go fishing."

Carly swung her head from side to side. "Not me," she said. She poked a finger out the kitchen window. "Him."

Malena looked out the window and back at Carly. "You want me to ask your neighbor to go fishing with us?"

"Absolutely. If he's fishing, I can work. Take him, please, only you don't have to ask him. I'll do it for you."

"Does he like fishing?"

"I'm sure he does. I saw his gear when I took him the cake. He's got it stashed on his porch."

Malena glanced out the window again. She lifted her shoulders and let them fall. "Okay, why not? I'll stick him with Ginny. He'll end up hating me, but I don't have to live next door to him."

"Then I'll ask him. You're going to Catwood Lake, aren't you?"

Malena nodded.

"They just finished that big dock that is accessible for wheelchairs. I'm sure Dev will have a good time, Ginny or no Ginny." Carly looked out the window as Dev came out on the porch. "I'll go over there later today and ask him. I'll call tonight and give you his answer."

Malena washed her hands and dried them. "Sounds great. Tell him I'll pick him up around ten. We're taking Hector's van."

Carly followed Malena to the front door. Prints, who had been lazily sitting in the sun pouring through the dining room window, joined the two ladies.

Carly told her cousin goodbye and let both Malena and Prints out the front door.

She went back to work. It was after five, and Meka had packed up her truck and left. Time to take advantage of the quiet again.

A couple of hours later, Dev fired up his woodworking tools. This time the sound didn't aggravate Carly. It reminded her she needed to talk to her neighbor and invite him on tomorrow's fishing trip.

How was she going to go about inviting him? She couldn't just run over there and ask him. She had to be subtle. She had to ask him in a way that would make him say yes.

She walked to the kitchen to get a glass of water

while she thought of a way to approach Dev. As she took a long, cool drink, she glanced around the room. Prints' food dish sat empty at one end of the kitchen. She'd forgotten to feed him, and she'd left him outside for hours, ever since Malena had left. She had to find the curious golden retriever at once.

She slipped into some sandals and went outside. "Prints," she called, but he couldn't possibly hear her over the noise from next door. "Prints."

She checked the garage and the doghouse, Prints' two favorite haunts. No sign of him. She walked up the street and called for him, but he didn't come.

She asked a couple of neighborhood boys, blond-haired, blue-eyed brothers, if they'd seen her dog. They hadn't.

She looked everywhere—except Devin's. All of a sudden, she realized her missing dog was her ticket to see Dev. Whether he'd seen Prints or not, she'd have the opportunity to ask him to go fishing with Malena and her friends and win herself a quiet few hours to work while he was gone.

She walked determinedly across her yard and into Dev's. She rounded the corner of his garage and held her hands over her ears to block out some of the screech of whatever power tool he was exercising at the moment. Dev was totally unaware of anything around him as he concentrated intently.

Carly stared at him long and hard. Even wearing his awkward safety glasses, sawdust speckling his hair, he was one great-looking guy. While he took his time to notice her presence, she admired his.

Dev carefully eyed the small block of wood through

his safety glasses. Once more around on the band saw, and its shape should be perfect. With the precision of a master, Dev finished cutting the little piece of pine. He switched the band saw off. Immediately, Prints left his side and ran toward the large door opening.

Dev looked up and saw what he'd been hoping to see ever since Prints showed up a couple of hours ago. He smiled at Carly as she held her hands over her ears. He took off his safety glasses and removed his hearing protection. "Good evening. What can I do for you?"

Carly let her hands fall to her sides. "I was looking for Prints."

Dev wheeled toward her. "He's been keeping me company."

Carly leaned over to pet her dog, then stood upright. "He usually doesn't run off like this."

"He doesn't?" *Probably because none of her previous neighbors called him over and gave him a hot dog or two.*

"No. He's real good about staying in the yard. He loves to laze on the porch."

Dev tilted his head as he wheeled a little closer to her. He wanted a better look at those bewitching eyes. "That's what porches are for. Maybe we could take a lesson from him."

She sent him a half grin that turned her eyes a soft sort of foamy sea blue. "Are you saying we should indulge in more leisure?"

He had to get closer still. Yes, foamy sea blue. Definitely. A playful, passionate, adventurous blue. "That's exactly what I'm saying." He pressed his elbows into the arms of his chair and laced his fingers in front of him. "What do you do to relax, Miss Ross?"

"I don't need to relax. I love to work."

"So do I, but no matter how much we enjoy our work, we still need time to do nothing or at least something entirely different from our routine."

"Oh?" she said, lifting a coy brow. Was she flirting with him? Something definitely looked different about her. "What do you do to break out of your routine, Mr. Serrano?"

"Me?" Dev replied, pressing his linked fingers into his chest. He shrugged. "When I was ironworking, I used to woodwork for relaxation."

"But you do that all the time," she said. She seemed angry, but she quickly pushed the emotion aside. She flung her hair over her shoulders. "I mean, you said you need to do something different, and you seem to spend a lot of time woodworking."

"I do now. That's true." He shifted in his chair. "Before the accident I used to hike and fish. I even went rock climbing a few times in the Wisconsin Dells area."

"I guess you'll have to wait to rock climb until you're totally healed, but some of the state parks have hiking trails that accommodate wheelchairs." She seemed to be trying to work her way around to something.

"I guess they do," he said, studying her and trying to read where she might be trying to lead him.

"One of the lakes nearby, Catwood Lake, even has a brand-new dock specially made for wheelchair access. It's a great place to go fishing."

Could it be that the two of them actually shared a recreational interest? "Fishing?"

"You just said you like fishing, and I noticed some gear on the front porch the day I brought you the cake." She squatted next to Prints and put her arm around him.

Dev moved closer to her, within inches. Her eyes, lower than his now, started to turn that darker color again. "What about it?"

"The fishing?" she asked, looking up at him.

He gave her a crooked nod and tried to read her eyes.

"I have a friend who loves fishing. She's going tomorrow with a couple of people she works with. She asked me if I'd like to go along, and I told her that maybe you'd like to go. As I said, I'd seen your gear on the porch, and I knew they had built that big dock." The dog nudged her, throwing her off balance, and she put her hand on Dev's chair to steady herself. "So what do you say? Do you want to go?"

He raised a hand to his face and rubbed it over his heavy beard to cover the delighted grin that insisted on brightening his face. She was asking him for a date. When he'd pushed the smile aside, he removed his hand. "Sounds great," he said.

"Good." She stood and took a step backward. "Malena will bring the food, but you can bring something to drink."

He wheeled forward. "Okay. What time are we going?"

She regressed a little farther. "Malena said she'd be here at ten."

"I'll look forward to it, then," he said, inching a little closer.

Carly stepped back out of the garage and glanced

toward her house. "I'd better get Prints home and feed him."

"Come here, Prints," Dev said, reaching toward the dog. Prints came to him immediately. He pet the retriever, then let him go. "I'll see you tomorrow at ten," he told Carly.

She was starting to walk away, but stopped abruptly and spun around. "Oh, I won't be going with you. I hate fishing. That's why Malena had room for you. Besides, I've got too much work to do." With that said, she whirled away from him and dashed home, leaving Dev in a cloud of confusion.

He sat back in his chair and wondered what had just happened. He couldn't believe he'd read her so inaccurately. Dev decided he must have been right in his earlier assessment of the beautiful Miss Carly Ross. She was all career. And maybe that was okay. He should be concentrating on his recovery and his art, not on getting to know his neighbor.

He wheeled out of the garage onto the driveway. He looked at her house and caught her staring out the window in his direction. All at once, she scurried out of sight. He smiled. She could back off all she wanted, but she was interested in him, whether she wanted to show it or not. One day, he'd break through her barriers and find the secret that lay behind those provocative eyes, no matter how much it complicated his life. Miss Carly Ross was simply too intriguing to ignore.

Chapter Six

Carly couldn't think of anything but her clever ploy to get Dev out of the house for a few hours. She had to get out into the yard and become a part of the events that were about to unfold.

She tucked her sleeveless gold and white shirt into her denim shorts, put on a pair of white socks, and laced up her white sneakers. She donned her ultraviolet eye protection and put a brimmed straw hat on her head, tucking her hair inside it.

Something had been gnawing on two of the bushes near the property line that edged her and Dev's yards. Now was the perfect time to kill the pests and insert herself inconspicuously into the events that would soon take place in Dev's yard.

Malena pulled into Dev's driveway as Carly examined her lilac bushes. These late bloomers showed a slight infestation of lilac borer. Meka had told her a couple of weeks earlier that it was important to treat the shrubs with insecticide before the flowers opened.

"Hey, cuz," Malena called as she stepped out of the van. She walked to Carly. "I thought you had to work today."

Carly turned to her cousin and took off her sunglasses. "I do. I'm just taking a few minutes to get rid of a pest or two."

Malena flicked her eyes toward Dev, who had suddenly appeared on the porch. When she looked back at Carly her dark eyes questioned Carly's words. "Meaning?"

Carly poked her thumb over her shoulder. "My lilacs have bugs." Her eyes left Malena and drew like a magnet to her neighbor. "Looks like Dev is ready. You guys can get underway."

Hector left the full-size navy blue van to help Dev with his gear.

"Guess so," Malena said, glancing at the activity behind her, then at Carly.

Carly leaned back on one foot and folded her arms, holding the insecticide in her right hand. "I'm glad you agreed to take Dev with you. He seemed real excited about going when I asked him yesterday. It'll be good for him to get out. I don't think he has too much company either. Even if Ginny is long-winded, I'm sure he'll enjoy having a little companionship today."

"You really think it would be good for him to be with a group of people, huh?"

"Sure. And foursomes are the perfect size, especially when it's boy, girl, boy, girl."

Malena glanced over her shoulder again and back at Carly. "You mean that?"

Carly shrugged and wondered why her cousin was

making such a point of something so trivial. "Of course."

Suddenly Malena grabbed the can of insecticide from Carly's hand and tossed it inside one of the infested lilac bushes. "The bugs will have to lick the can until we get back," she said, taking Carly's arm.

"What?" Carly asked incredulously.

Malena tugged at her arm. "I said the bugs can wait. You're going fishing. Ginny had to cancel out on us, so we're missing one of the girls from our boy, girl, boy, girl. You'll have to fill in to complete the foursome."

Carly yanked her arm away. "Wait a minute. I'm not going fishing. I hate fishing."

Malena took Carly's arm again and dragged her toward the van. "It's too late for that. You made your case, and I bought it. You're going fishing with us."

Dev and Hector were on the other side of the van when Carly and Malena reached it. Each of the men opened their doors and got inside.

Malena slid the back door of the van open. "Get in, Carly."

Carly slid the door shut. "I'm not going," she whispered.

Malena flung the door open again. "Hi, Dev, I'm Malena Sanchez," she said, sticking out the hand that wasn't latched to Carly's arm.

Dev shook her hand. "Devin Serrano. Nice to meet you." He moved his eyes from Malena to Carly. "Are you coming after all?" He grinned toward her.

Carly shook her head, but she said, "I guess so."

"Then let's go," Malena said, moving Carly's arm to urge her into the van.

Carly stepped up. She seated herself on the soft leather bench seat next to Dev.

Malena slid into the front captain's chair and introduced Hector to their passengers.

"Glad to have you aboard," Hector said, nodding his head hard enough to shake his red curls. His light blue eyes twinkled. "I hope you like to fish. I hear they're really biting at Catwood." He turned back and glanced at Dev in the rearview mirror. "Ever been there?"

"Not yet," Dev said, looking at Hector's reflection in the mirror. "I'm looking forward to it." He turned to Carly and curled the corners of his mouth. "Even more so now."

Carly forced her eyes away from him. She looked out the window on her side.

Cruising up the street and out onto the highway, Hector brought up the various species of fish that lived in Catwood Lake.

Carly was relieved to have the three fishermen discussing a subject she could steer clear of. Sitting next to Dev was throwing off her equilibrium. She was afraid if she'd been required to engage in conversation, whatever she'd say might come out garbled.

"What made you change your mind?" Dev's voice came from behind.

Carly tore her eyes from the scenery speeding by the side window and looked at him. "Excuse me?"

"About going fishing. You said you hate to fish. Why did you decide to come along?" He sent her a half-smile and tucked a stray strand of hair behind her ear, letting his finger linger on her lobe.

Carly moved her head, tugging her ear away from

his burning touch. "I'm not sure. Ginny Michaels was supposed to go, but she couldn't make it. Malena wanted me to take her place." She tried to pull her eyes from the dark ones above her, but they refused to move.

He touched another stray strand of blond and toyed with it carefully as he leveled her with his dark gaze. Suddenly, he dropped his probing fingers and glanced out the window to his side. He looked back at Carly. "It's a beautiful day, cool and sunny." He cocked his head and gave her another half-smile. "Despite the fact that you hate to fish, I think you'll manage to have a nice time." His eyes moved to the outdoors again before they returned to her. "Who wouldn't on such a lovely day?"

Hector pulled into a parking spot near the lake and turned off the van.

As the foursome exited the van, Carly had to admit Dev was right about one thing. It was a lovely day. Perhaps a little tryst with nature would refresh her and stir her productive capabilities. A little revitalization might be just what she needed to spur on her creative energy and move her production rate into hyperspeed.

Whatever the impending result of spending the day in the fresh air and sunshine, she might as well enjoy herself. She wasn't going anywhere for at least a few hours.

All four of them fished from the large dock for more than an hour without any luck. Dev wasn't used to not catching anything, but this time he didn't mind. It was far too amusing watching Carly's antics as she tried to manage a fiberglass rod and reel. He'd never seen anything so comical in his life. If he'd caught her on tape, a producer would have accused him of stealing from the Keystone Kops, the Three Stooges, and Charlie Chaplin all at once, not to mention Lucy Ricardo and Ethel Mertz.

Carly wasn't exactly the quietest fisherman he'd ever cast a line with either. Hector sent a poisoned gaze her way several times. Each threatening look he threw at Carly was loaded with enough disdain that Dev was ready to stand and walk over to the skinny carrot-top and punch him in the nose. This was one of the few times he cursed his current inability to function fully, even though he'd never actually hit a man so much smaller than him without adequate provocation.

One more of those looks, though, just might be provoking enough.

"Malena," Dev called, "I thought the fishing was suppose to be good here. Where are all the fish?"

She looked at Dev and shrugged as she reeled in her line. "Maybe there are too many of us here. We might be scaring away the fish."

"Yes," Hector said, tossing another frustrated glance in Carly's direction. He looked at Malena. "Why don't we try another spot?"

Yes, Dev thought, *why don't you.*

"You want to?" Malena asked, bending to pick up her tackle box.

Hector finished reeling in his line. "Wouldn't hurt."

Malena glanced at Dev, Carly, then back at Hector. "I know a little cove that way," she said, pointing, "where the crappies are suppose to be biting. You and I could go there . . ." She looked again at Carly, then

Dev. ". . . if you don't mind the two of us going off by ourselves."

"Not at all," Dev replied without allowing Carly to offer an opinion. He certainly wasn't going to give his neighbor an opportunity to object to Malena's suggestion.

Carly cast a scornful look at Dev, then let her eyes drift to meet Malena's. "Sure, go ahead. You two might as well catch something. I'm afraid the only way I'd bring in a fish would be to have a diver hang one on my line."

Dev stifled the giant laugh that pounded against his ribs. The lady was right. She might know engineering, but she knew less about fishing than a baby spider knew about building an airplane.

Hector tucked his gear under one arm and draped the other around Malena's shoulders. "We'll be back later," he called as they walked away. Then, smiling at them over Malena's head, he said, "With a stringer full of crappies."

Dev watched the thin young man, dressed in dark blue cotton shorts and a white *Get Hooked on Fishing* T-shirt, stroll away with Carly's gorgeous friend. Turning his attention to Carly, he asked, "Have you and Malena been friends long?"

Carly pulled her line out of the water and worked on her tenth tangled line of the day. "Friends?" she repeated, concentrating on her line.

"Bring that here," Dev said, putting his fiberglass rod aside.

Carly took her rod and reel to him and turned it over. She took a step back and removed her sunglasses.

Dev pulled a knife from the tackle box next to his chair and cut the line. Then he fixed the hook, weight, and floater at the proper places on Carly's line. "What about you and Malena, have you been friends long?"

Carly tilted her head. "All our lives. We're cousins."

Dev's eyes snapped up to meet hers. "Cousins? You don't look anything alike. And didn't she say when she introduced herself her name was Sanchez?"

"My mother, Mariana, is the sister of Malena's dad, Joe. As for not looking alike, you're right. But that's not unusual. Not with cousins. Sometimes even with brothers and sisters. My mother is much fairer-skinned than her brother Joe, but her eyes are darker than Malena's. Uncle Joe's rather swarthy, yet he has light blue eyes. I guess we're a mixed mass of the human genome."

"Well, nature has created some of its most beautiful art in you," he said, grinning at her.

Carly's cheeks turned crimson.

"And your cousin," Dev added wryly.

The blush left her cheeks, and she yanked her fishing gear from his grasp. "You won't mind if I fish at the other end of the dock, will you?"

He picked up the pole he had laid next to his chair and wheeled closer to her. "Did I say something wrong?"

She blew out a deep breath and shook her head. "No." She looked out at the lake and put her sunglasses back on. "I guess I'm a little frustrated." She turned back to him. "I told you I hate fishing. I'm terrible at it."

Dev gazed up at her. "Would you like some help?"

Carly swished her head from side to side. "There's no point. I'm hopeless."

Dev gave a sudden yank on his fishing rod. He began to reel in his line.

"You've got something!" Carly exclaimed, thrusting her eyes toward the lake.

Carefully, Dev played his catch, letting it run with the line, then reeling it in when its fight subsided. Within minutes he netted a two-pound walleye. "Mmm—mmm," Dev commented, "he'll be good to eat."

"It's about time one of us had some luck," Carly said over a chuckle of delight.

Dev glanced up at her. "Want to try again?" He thought the thrill of the catch might intrigue her enough not to give up just yet.

She lifted a shoulder and raised a brow. "Why not?"

Dev helped her bait her hook and showed her an easy way to cast her line.

Her first few efforts were as clumsy as they'd been all day, but her fifth cast was effective. With her line finally planted in the water, maybe she'd have some luck.

Dev sent his own freshly baited line to its mark. "What kind of projects do you work on, Carly?"

"Engineering?"

"Yes."

She stared at her floater as though she'd miss a glimpse of the president if she looked away. "I've been doing consulting and small structural projects for all kinds of companies in the area. I do a few consults for private people too." She leaned one way, then the other, staring at the red and white bobber. "I'm trying to get into high-rise projects. They're the most lucrative."

It seemed that if she was distracted enough, she could go on about work all day. "So your career goal is to become wealthy?"

Suddenly her head snapped round to him, and she ripped the shades from her eyes and shoved them into her pocket. "Wealthy?" She wiped her wrist over her upper lip. "A little wealth never hurt, but I wouldn't say it is my ultimate goal. What I really hope to accomplish is the building of an excellent reputation. Then businesses will come after me, and I will no longer have to court them. I won't have to work night and day on some spec project that might all turn out to be a waste of time."

Dev hadn't meant to upset her, but it looked as though that was exactly what he'd done.

Carly swung the arm that didn't hold the fishing rod. "Which is precisely what I should be working on right now—my projects. I've got no business standing on a dock staring at a piece of plastic floating on a lake." She swung her arm again. This time she lost her balance.

Dev instantly reached for her hand and pulled her from the edge of the dock. "Careful. It's a lovely day for a swim, but I'll bet that water is still a little cold."

Carly yanked her hand from his. She turned back to the lake and began to reel in her line.

Dev wheeled a few feet away from her and moved his line so it would not become entangled with hers.

She deftly finished reeling and secured her line. She turned to walk down the dock and promptly tripped over Dev's tackle box.

He'd left it right in her way. In a flash he was next to Carly. He reached for her and hoisted her onto his lap. "Are you all right?"

She clutched her knee and scrunched up her face. "No, I am not all right. I hurt my knee."

She pushed against him, but he held her fast. "Hold on, Graceful, you're not going anywhere."

She squirmed and challenged him a while longer until she silently relented. Then she settled against him and rubbed her knee. "Ow."

"Let me take a look," Dev said, pushing her hand aside. Gently he raised her leg. He took off his sunglasses and examined her bruise. "I'd say you're going to have a colorful palette on the patella, but you'll be okay."

She snatched her leg from his grasp and tried to get off his lap. "Let me go."

He pulled her back against him. "Don't be silly. I'm sure you're not seriously hurt, but it will be quite painful to walk on that leg for a while."

With one more shove against his massive chest, Carly set herself free. She took two steps and went down like a wounded deer.

Dev wheeled next to her and lifted her back to his lap. Without verbalizing the *I told you so* pounding against his teeth, he grabbed the tackle box and started rolling down the long deck back to shore.

Carly snuggled against him, rubbing her knee and grimacing.

Dev rolled over each board on the dock slowly and deliberately. He was in no hurry to return to the van. He might never have a chance to hold her again. If only he didn't need both of his hands to maneuver his chair. He'd love to wrap an arm around her, securing her to him, feeling her heartbeat, touching the softness of her skin. But that was not an option.

Suddenly, a tear trickled from Carly's eye. The sight of it brought Dev to a dead stop. He took hold of Carly's shoulders and pulled her back from him.

She winced in pain and looked away.

His heart began to race. "You're really hurting, aren't you?"

She lifted her eyes to meet his. "I told you I was."

He had no idea she hurt so bad. And here he had been selfishly taking his time at getting her back to the van. "I'm sorry," he said, lifting his fingers to her chin. "We'll get some ice on that knee immediately." With both hands firmly on his wheels, he nearly left skid marks on the deck as he wheeled over it. Within seconds they were at the van. Dev helped Carly into the bench seat where they sat together on the ride from Pine Grove, then got ice for her knee. He wrapped it in a cloth napkin, climbed in next to her, and applied the compress. He slid his arm over the top of the seat. "Feel better?" he asked, leaning close to her.

She looked up at him, her eyes wet and shining, the whites of them like lights around the darkness of a tunnel. "I'm fine," she said, forcing a smile. "I told you I'm no good at fishing."

Chapter Seven

Dev smiled at her show of courage.

Carly looked deeply into his eyes and tried to discern which was more painful, her injured knee or the longing Dev ignited in the depths of her soul whenever he was close to her. She blinked to break his spell and dragged her eyes from his. She lay her head back against the soft black leather.

Dev raised the compress and examined Carly's knee. "It doesn't seem to be swelling, but a bump on a bone like that can really hurt." He replaced the icepack and looked back at Carly.

She winced as the coldness touched her knee once more, then opened her eyes. For a few seconds, Carly could have sworn she saw true concern written in his expression.

Then, keeping one hand on the icepack over Carly's knee, Dev rested his other arm along the back of the seat behind her. He inclined his head toward her. "A while ago, you said you were working on a project for a high-rise. How is that going?"

Carly cringed as the mention of her work seemed to intensify the pain in her leg. "Not very well." She looked away. "I'm having trouble concentrating." She wanted to add "because you're making so much noise," but she couldn't afford to insult him now while he held her knee in his hand. Besides, she didn't resent him at the moment either. She was far too attracted to him for that.

"Maybe you work too hard."

She bolted up in her seat, then regretted the sudden move as pain streaked up and down her leg. "Ooo, ow!" she wailed.

Dev gently urged her back into her seat. "Sit still. You've got to give it a little time for the ice to take effect."

She leaned back and relaxed as much as she could with pain coursing through her leg and desire wreaking havoc on her senses.

Dev's dark eyes brightened. "Do you know the man who lives on the other side of me?"

Carly smiled at the mention of Dev's sweet, senile neighbor. "Mr. Cosgrove? Of course."

"He's sort of a strange one, isn't he?"

She shook her head. "Not strange, just old."

"He does look like he could have voted for McKinley. I guess that's why he has such a poor memory. Every time he sees me, he threatens me with a wooden bat. He thinks I'm a prowler casing Mrs. Applebee's house."

Carly chuckled. "He was very protective of Mrs. Applebee before she passed away. They lived next door to each other for over thirty years. In his elderly confusion, I suppose he still thinks she lives in your house."

Dev tilted his head and grinned at her. "You don't think he'd ever actually use that bat on me do you?"

Carly grinned back at him. "You never know. He liked Mrs. Applebee very much. I think he was in love with her." She looked at Dev carefully. His eyes drifted over her face as though he were studying her, searching for something. "You aren't worried, are you?"

His brows crept together. "Worried?" The hand resting on the top of the seat moved and knocked the brimmed hat from Carly's head.

A mass of soft, blond curls fell around her face and across Dev's arm. Carly rounded her lips into a surprised circle and brushed a lock from her face.

Dev drew in a sudden breath and his eyes grew darker than midnight. His fingers slipped into Carly's hair and gently caressed her scalp.

His nearness and scent alone were enough to completely dismantle her defenses. This sensual touch would undo her completely if she didn't make an effort to move away from him.

Carly pressed a hand to his chest to push herself away from him, but she didn't move.

Instead, Dev came closer, taking possession of her with his evocative eyes and twisting his fingers in her hair.

Carly opened the fingers of the hand pressing against Dev's powerful chest. The steely sinew there roused her curiosity further, and she slid her hand slowly upwards, covering a mass of muscle over the ribs beneath the dark T-shirt. More meandering led her to his collarbone, then the back of his neck.

Dev closed his eyes as she touched his nape and dragged in a ragged breath. He opened them once more and stared into her soul.

Totally exposed to him, she was compelled to complete their connection. She pressed against his neck, moving him closer to her, focusing on his provocative eyes, concentrating on taking a piece of him for herself. Nothing else mattered but becoming a part of him.

The hand in her hair cupped the back of her head as Dev's gaze fastened on her, anticipating what was to come.

Her fingers at his neck pulling him closer, Carly lifted her face to his. One last inquiry into the irresistible eyes, then lids fell and lips met. An unknown joy coursed through her and she shivered.

Dev dropped the compress he'd continued to hold at her knee and moved his hand up her leg until it rested at her waist.

Carly moved her free hand to join the one at the back of Dev's neck, urging him to kiss her more deeply. She could have spent the rest of her life kissing Dev. In the rapture of the moment, she didn't care if she ever breathed again. She wanted only him, to be a part of him and to dwell within the bliss he offered in the most extraordinary kiss she'd ever known.

Drawing her closer still, Dev's lips left hers only long enough to taste her cheeks and eyes and forehead before regaining access to her eager mouth.

With every second the kiss grew, her heart magnified, and her need for him drowned her with desire.

Like an echo from the bottom of a cavern, Carly's name intruded on her fantasy. She stirred and murmured against his lips as she tried to respond.

She heard her name again, louder this time, sounding more real.

"Carly!" Malena shouted.

She yanked herself from his arms and threw her gaze out the open window behind her. Malena and Hector were coming. She flashed her glance back at Dev. Her eyes darted from him to her lap and back to him. Her wrist popped to her mouth, then drew away. "I'm sorry," she said, "I'm so sorry. I never should have . . ." She squared her shoulders and tucked in her loosened shirt, then looked back up at him. "It won't ever happen again."

He took hold of her wrist as she tried to reach for the door and gave her a sardonic smile. "I didn't mind."

Frustrated by his cavalier attitude, she snatched her wrist from him. "Malena's calling me." She reached for the door again.

Once more he seized her arm. "You're not going anywhere," he said in the huskiest voice she'd ever heard.

She tugged her arm, but he didn't release it.

"Did you forget about your injury?" he asked with a wry grin.

She had forgotten. The second he mentioned it, the pain returned. She bent to pick up the compress and placed it on the offending knee.

Within seconds Malena was at the van. She held up a stringer of eight crappies. "Guess we got enough for dinner." She swung open the van door. As soon as she saw the ice pack on Carly's knee, she said, "Honey, what happened?"

"I fell and hurt my knee."

"Let me see," Malena said, taking a look. She shook her head. "Bet it hurts, huh?" She glanced up at her cousin. "And you're getting overheated, too, sitting in this van. You're all flushed."

Carly dropped the compress as her hands sprang to her face, and her cheeks grew even warmer. Luckily Malena hadn't guessed the real reason for her rosy glow.

"We'd better get you right home," Malena said. "You've got to get your feet up." She looked Carly in the eye one more time and shook her head. "And we've got to get you out of the heat." Malena closed the door and shouted for Hector, who was still twenty yards away.

As Malena put the fish in the back and walked around to the passenger side of the vehicle, Dev looked Carly over carefully. "I think the heat has done wonders for you," he teased. Then, in the most serious tone she'd ever heard from him, he said, "You're even more beautiful than before." He gently touched her cheek and stared at her hard.

Carly gulped and shuddered. She was sure that in a moment she would urge him to kiss her once more. Suddenly, she regained control and batted his hand away. "Stop that, and don't ever mention what happened here again. I've never made a bigger mistake in my life. I wish the whole thing never happened."

He tossed her another derisive grin. "You could have fooled me."

The drive home took an eternity. Carly toyed with

the idea of forcing Dev out of her seat and making him sit in the chair in the back, but she didn't want to do anything that would raise Hector's and Malena's suspicions. Dev's wry, contemptuous attitude had aggravated her, and his constant nearness continued to rattle her senses. She needed to be away from him— or back in his arms. Neither choice was a possibility at the moment.

Hector pulled into Carly's driveway and parked the van. He turned round and said, "Sit tight, Carly. I'll help you inside."

The last thing Carly wanted was to take Hector's sensible advice. She wanted to fling the van door open and run into the sanctuary of her home. She had to be away from Devin Serrano as soon as possible. Unfortunately, the quickest way to make a successful exit was to do exactly as Hector suggested.

Carly's door swung open, and she slid to the edge of her seat. Hector reached for her, placing his hands around her waist. He lifted her down.

She stood on both legs, leaning into his side. Two unsteady steps later she felt herself being swept up in Hector's arms.

"Let's do this the easy way," he told her. "It'd be better if you didn't put any weight on that knee for a couple of hours."

Dev sat forward and cursed his weak legs almost as enthusiastically as he condemned Hector for taking Carly into his arms. Never mind the fact that the skinny computer man did exactly the right thing to get her into the house safely. Hector had no right to pick her up like that.

As he watched Malena follow Hector and Carly up

the steps to the porch and front door, Dev leaned back in his seat. He hadn't any right himself to take Carly into his arms, yet he'd done it—and not for the noble reason Hector had.

He'd seized an opportunity, and, if it had been solely up to him, he'd have never let go. Carly became a part of him the instant their lips touched. When she tore herself away, he felt as though he'd lost a vital organ. When she told him she was sorry, called what they'd done the biggest mistake of her life, she'd stolen his spirit.

But those moments of union, breathing as one, holding each other, touching, learning, melding together, those were worth whatever it cost, and he'd never regret them—even if he lived to be as old as Mr. Cosgrove.

Hector returned a few minutes after he took Carly into the house. He told Dev Malena was staying with Carly to take care of her. Then he drove Dev next door to his house.

As Dev cleaned the walleye and fried it for his dinner, he wished Carly could share the catch with him. He glanced out the window toward her house while he ate and wondered how she was doing. He'd call her and ask, but he didn't want to upset her. She'd been pretty clear about regretting what she'd done and emphatic in her attempt to put some distance between them.

If he hoped to ever have contact with her again, he'd better give her the space she needed.

When dinner was finished and the dishes were put away, Dev headed to the shop in the garage. After a

minute he angled away from the workshop and instead
turned his chair toward the studio.

The day's events had sharpened his senses and stim-
ulated his imagination. This acute awareness would be
much better used in front of a canvas than over a
power tool. He took the sketch pad, pencils and paints
he needed, and set to his task.

Over the next few weeks silence resonated from
Dev's garage for all but a couple of hours a day.
Though Carly was completing her smaller projects in
record time and moving ahead on the Montgomery
proposal, she couldn't help worrying that something
might be wrong with her neighbor. She nearly closed
the distance between the two of them several times to
make sure Dev was all right, but she knew she couldn't
afford the distraction and vulnerability that might overcome her again in his presence. Besides, she was getting what she wanted: enough quiet to work effectively.
Why risk losing that?

Client calls started to increase, and Carly found herself with more work than she could handle and still
have time to continue the Montgomery project. Re-
grettably, she had to put people off until after the Sep-
tember deadline for the high-rise proposal.

As July began, Carly had no choice but to put
everything aside to concentrate on the Montgomery
proposition exclusively. She wanted to be seriously
considered for the career-making opportunity of a lifetime.

She'd no more than pulled up one of the Montgomery CAD designs when a router started to scream next
door. Hoping that this episode in the workshop would

be short-lived, as had been the case recently, Carly ignored the noise as best she could and continued to work.

Dev's clamorous activity continued the rest of the day and filled the remainder of the week.

It was time to send a new prospect to Devin's house. He had shown no interest in Meka Tanabe. Maybe she was too short for him, as Carly had originally suspected. Luckily, his house needed painting badly, and Carly had just the craftsman for him. Cammie Lundgren was every bit as beautiful as Meka, but she was a very different woman. Cammie moved her tall, slender, statuesque body with the grace of a swan. Her straight, dark-blond hair hung to the middle of her back even when drawn up in a ponytail. Her deep blue eyes emitted a confidence and warmth that made everyone feel like an instant companion. And, even though she usually wore jeans and a plain blue workshirt, the beholder would have sworn by the way she moved that she was dressed in the most elegant of gowns.

Perhaps a strong, assertive man like Dev would find the shy but confident Cammie the perfect mate.

That twinge twisted under Carly's ribs again, and she massaged it away.

Maybe Cammie wouldn't be the perfect mate. Carly didn't care if Dev got married. In fact, she preferred he didn't. She just wanted him to quiet down again. Getting his mind off woodworking and on Cammie could do just that.

It took two weeks for Cammie to start work on Dev's house—fourteen days that made Carly wish she was living next to a family of eleven children and a dozen dogs so she'd have a little more quiet.

Cammie finally arrived and began work. Carly watched Dev and the house painter interact, hoping to see some flicker of interest in her neighbor's expression. But it was business as usual. Dev went back to the garage and sent shrieking sounds through the neighborhood, and Cammie started assembling metal scaffolding, hammering, clanging, banging.

Cammie's extreme efficiency allowed her to finish her job in just over a week, but, when she left, it was for good. Strike two. Dev showed no interest in her either.

Time for prospect number three. But who would it be? Dev's yard was in tip-top shape, thanks to Meka, and Cammie had turned his house into one of the most impressive in the neighborhood.

Dev had said he was thinking about remodeling his house, but all the home remodelers Carly knew were men.

Finding another woman for Dev wouldn't be easy. To her surprise, Carly felt a sense of satisfaction in that realization.

A quiet morning a few days after Cammie finished her job allowed Carly a highly productive start to her day. She became so engrossed in her work she forgot she'd let Prints out after breakfast. She looked for him at lunchtime, but she didn't find him. Her work beckoned her, so she decided to search for her dog later. He'd be fine. He always was.

By three, Prints had still not returned. Carly decided she'd better get out and look for the curious canine. She tucked the off-white peasant blouse into her gauzy gold and blue skirt and donned a pair of sandals. She went out into the yard and began to call Prints by name.

She walked all the way around the house, checking the empty garage and kennel, before she found her lazy dog dozing under the maple tree that grew on the property line she shared with Dev. Carly roused him, and the dog jumped to his feet, circling her enthusiastically. Taking hold of his collar, Carly steadied Prints so she could pet him. She scolded him as she stroked him. When she let him go, he circled her once more, then ran off.

Carly called after him. "Prints, come back here this instant."

He paid no attention to her. Instead, he tore up the grass, running over Dev's driveway and sidewalk and bounding up the ramp until he reached the front door. Giving one look in Carly's direction as though he were making sure she was following him, Prints tore inside the door Dev had left ajar.

Ten seconds later, Carly was inside Dev's living room. The instant she planted her feet on his scratched, hardwood floor she realized she had intruded without knocking. She opened her mouth to speak but stopped when she heard Dev's soothing voice.

"Prints, are you here again? Do you want something else to eat?"

Carly followed the husky sound to a small room off the living room. Dev sat in his wheelchair stroking Prints' fur. She folded her arms and leaned against the door jamb. "Does he want something to eat?"

Dev's eyes snapped toward her. "Carly! I didn't hear you come in."

Feeling suddenly uneasy at her breech of etiquette,

she stammered, "The front door was open. Prints ran inside. I came after him." She shook her head. "I'm sorry I didn't knock."

Dev nervously spun his chair around and held his arm toward the living room. "Let's go sit down and talk. I haven't seen you for a while."

His restlessness puzzled her. Dev was never ill at ease. He was the most self-assured man she knew. "Is anything wrong?"

He forced his face into a half-smile. "No, of course not. What could be wrong?"

She didn't buy his denial. She intended to press him further, as she suspected Prints might have done something he shouldn't have. She was responsible for him, and if he had damaged some of Dev's property, she'd take care of it. She started to ask him again what was wrong when something unusual caught her eye.

She immediately straightened her stance and dropped her arms. She stepped carefully into his studio. "Why, Dev," she said, staring at the canvas he'd been working on, "you're an artist." She moved closer to his painting. She reached her hand toward it, then pulled it back. She pressed her fingers to her lips and turned to meet his eyes. Her gaze filled with awe, she moved her fingers away from her mouth. "I don't believe it."

He pressed his elbows into the arms of his chair and laced his fingers together. He cocked his head and scrunched his face over an impertinent smile. "That bad, huh?"

She turned back to the work on the canvas and reached toward it again. "Bad?" She stepped closer.

"It's absolutely breathtaking. I've never seen anything like it."

He wheeled next to her, studying what she scrutinized. "You think so?"

"Definitely." She nearly touched the texture. It drew her the way he did. "The perspective . . ." She twisted her head to find his eyes. "It's because you're an iron worker. You see things from high above and far away. That's why you paint as though you see beyond the subject to all the outside influences."

Dev lifted himself by his elbows, pinned into the arms of the chair, and shifted his weight. His eyes filled with a devilish twinkle. "For someone who claims to know nothing about art, you seem to know a lot about this piece of paint."

Carly glanced back at Dev's work, then at him. "Oh, I don't know anything about art, but I know what I see and how I feel." She looked at the painting again. "And this painting tells me a story, like the one over your fireplace."

Suddenly, Carly hunched down and rested with her ankles beneath her. Her hair fell loose around her shoulders. She put her hands on the arms of his chair and smiled up at him. "Dev, this is wonderful." She glanced around the room from her crouched position, then returned her eyes to his. "Can you show me more?"

His smile vanished, and his eyes grew very dark. "I can't think of anything I'd rather do."

Chapter Eight

W hat did he say? Dev couldn't believe he'd just offered to show Carly his work. No one on earth had seen it except Henry. Like Carly, Henry had discovered it by accident one day when he came to help Dev with his therapy. But Henry just helped himself to a look without asking permission. He was that kind of guy.

Carly asked to see more paintings, she didn't demand it. He could have said no. He should have said no. He wasn't ready for anyone to see his work, especially someone he cared about as much as he found himself caring about Carly.

But he couldn't refuse her anything when she caught him with those intriguing eyes. Sea blue today, bright, curious, glowing after she had noticed his painting.

He pulled Carly to her feet, keeping his eyes focused on hers. Then he wrenched his gaze from her

87

and stood. He took two unassisted steps to the table in the middle of the small room.

Carly threw her hands to her mouth, and her brows shot heavenward. "You're walking!"

Dev glanced at her and smiled at her shocked expression. "A few steps here and there. I've been working hard on my physical therapy lately. It's starting to pay off." He seated himself on the edge of the sturdy table.

Carly took an enthusiastic step toward him. She put her arms out and the next thing Dev knew he was swallowed up inside a soft embrace.

"I'm so happy for you," Carly said, giving him a grin he could have sworn was full of pride.

Just as he was about to stand and really take her into his arms, she let him go and turned to the painting on the wall behind her.

"Another scene from high above the ground," she said, thinking out loud. "More iron worker influence. I don't see a story in this one, only an observation."

Dev sat on the table and folded his arms. Let her look, he decided. While she's inspecting my art I can enjoy hers. He'd never seen anything more comely than Carly Ross: her long, flowing hair wild about her shoulders, the shapely legs hidden by the full skirt, the tiny waist he wanted to circle with his hands, and her eyes—he couldn't see them at the moment with her back to him, but he knew them well. The enthusiasm she exuded as she examined his paintings would put a twinkle inside the sea of blue and a shine like a reflection of sunbeams. He wanted to see it.

He'd no more than wished for a look into her eyes

when she turned around and gazed directly at him. "Did you hear me?"

Yes, they were sparkling like stars on the sea.

"Dev?"

He blinked. "What did you say?"

"I asked if this painting represented something you actually saw while you were working or if you made it up yourself?"

He knitted his brows and looked at her curiously. "Why would you ask that?"

She glanced back at the painting and then at him. "Because it seems so unusual, like it had to be real. No one would make it up."

"You think so?" For professing to be an amateur about art, Carly seemed to understand his work very well.

She returned her eyes to the painting. "In this part of the work," she said, pointing to the upper left quadrant, "there are streets clogged with traffic. It's very city-like. Even the colors suggest tension." She moved her finger to the upper right quadrant. "Here is a suburban neighborhood, mild traffic, but safe enough for kids on bikes and dogs running free." Her attention descended to the lower right quadrant. "There's nothing but a boy and a lake over here. He's fishing by himself, laying back on the ground, chewing on a blade of grass, waiting for his catch. It's the complete opposite of the other corner." She stared at the pastoral scene a moment longer, then commented on the remaining quadrant. "In this part of the painting, you've included a small piece of the building in the foreground from which all the perspective comes."

Lovely, smart, intuitive. Dev tried to keep his eyes

on the painting as she pointed out her observations, but it was impossible. There was only one work of art in the room that interested him at the moment.

Carly turned back to him. "You saw this one day while you were working, didn't you?"

He had to be closer to her. Right now. He stood and took the one step necessary to close the space between them. He stretched his hand to the wall and leaned into it, placing himself over Carly. Talk about a better perspective. He loved standing above her, her looking up at him. He wanted to touch her face, but he didn't want to scare her away.

"Didn't you?" she asked, her eyes beginning to darken.

"See the scene from my perch on top of a building?" he asked, staring down at her.

She blinked twice, and some of the darkness faded back to sea blue. "Yes."

Memory pushed away his momentary obsession with her. He closed his eyes and moved his head toward the painting she was talking about. When he looked at it, he curled his lips over his teeth solemnly and nodded his head. He drew in a deep breath and let it out slowly. "This is what I saw my last day on the job."

His gaze lingered on the painting as memories flooded his mind. In a few moments he filed them away where they belonged and turned back to Carly.

A tear trickled down her cheek as her eyes focused on his painting.

His free hand went immediately to her face, and he brushed the moisture away with his thumb. "My painting makes you weep?" He rubbed his finger over her cheek again. "I didn't mean to make anyone cry over my work."

She pressed her cheek into his hand, then looked up at him with glistening eyes. She shook her head. "I'm sorry. Sometimes I get a little too empathetic." She brushed his hand away and looked back at the painting. "You see, I know what it takes to design something that's living deep inside you, to put an idea on paper. And I know what it feels like to accomplish something as perfectly as you've done here," she said, inclining her head toward the picture. "I guess I'm sharing that deep sense of satisfaction, and I got a little emotional about it." She wiped her fingers over her cheeks and grinned up at him. "Sorry about that."

He touched a finger to her chin, then dropped his hand. "Forget it."

"Good," she said, giving her head one firm downward motion. "Let's take a look at the next one."

Dev followed her all the way around the room as she examined each of his paintings. While she admired them, he admired her. By the time she'd completed her inspection, his back and legs were weary, but he'd never felt more energized.

When she'd finished studying the last of his work, she turned to him. A look crossed her face that Dev judged to be part surprise, part fear, and part passion.

"Well?" he said, his voice deep and husky.

Her eyes shifted back and forth without leaving his. "Well . . . what?"

He moved a little closer, placing himself within inches of her. "Does my work pass inspection?"

She took a step back and found herself pressed against the wall. "It's breathtaking, Dev."

Dev stepped closer to her. He raised a hand above her and leaned into the wall to take some of the weight off his tired back and legs. "Breathtaking?" he asked, rubbing a finger along her jawbone.

Carly pressed her eyes shut. Her arms were stiff at her sides, the palms of her hands pressed into the wall.

Dev stared at her, drinking in her loveliness. He had to kiss her again as he'd done in the van. He needed to be close to her.

Carly lifted her lids slowly. She sent a steamy glimpse upwards. Her message was clear. If ever a woman wanted to be kissed . . .

Dev gently grasped her chin and moved toward her, staring at her waiting lips. In a moment, they'd be joined as they'd been before.

Suddenly, Carly drew in a deep breath. Her eyes grew to the size of grapefruits. "Prints!" she shouted.

Dev's hands froze in place, one on the wall above her and the other gently holding her face. He lifted his brows and said, "I beg your pardon?"

"Prints!" she said again. She drew up her hand and started to shake it. Her eyes fell to her right. "Stop that!"

Dev immediately stepped back to the table and sat down. "I'm sorry," he said, believing he had read her completely wrong and actually offended her. She seemed to be calling the dog on him.

She rubbed her hand back and forth on her skirt several times. "I hate it when he licks my hand like that. He always does it when he's hungry." She took hold of Prints' collar and stepped into the doorway. "I'd better get him home and feed him." She looked back at Dev. "Thanks for showing me your paintings. They're beautiful, Dev."

Before Dev could respond, she was out his front door. He sat at the table, arms folded, and shook his head. Then he looked through his doorway and said, "Thanks."

Amusement covered his face. He'd never seen such an enthusiastic exit. He must have lost his touch. If he couldn't hold the interest of a beautiful woman who'd come in to see his paintings, something must be wrong. Or maybe the lady fancied only the art and not the artist.

Either way, she was gone. Only that lovely lavender scent remained and the memory of the feel of her silken complexion against his hand. Considering the haste in which she left, Dev decided a long time would pass again before he saw Carly Ross.

He stood and moved to his wheelchair. As he was about to sit in it, he pushed it away. Never mind that his legs and back ached. He was on his feet, and he was going to stay that way for a while.

He walked through the doorway into the living room. He was a step away from the sofa when the front door swung open. The sudden motion startled him, causing his legs to give out beneath him. His gaze shot toward the doorway.

Carly dashed in and stood next to him. "Oh, I'm sorry. I made you fall." She took hold of the coffee table. "I'll just move this out of the way and help you up."

"That isn't necessary," he said, trying to get up on his own. But his legs were more weakened and tired than he'd thought.

Carly bent to move the coffee table and Prints butted into her. She fell into the table and rammed it into Dev's shin.

He grabbed his leg. "You really don't have to help, Carly. I can manage."

"No," she insisted, "it's my fault."

Prints butted against her, and she hammered Dev's shin again.

This time the pain doubled him over. "It was an accident," he said through gritted teeth. "It wasn't your fault. You don't need to help." Dev let go of his leg and tried to lift himself from the floor, pushing against it with his hands.

All the activity on the floor put Prints in a playful mood. He jumped on Dev's chest and his arms went out from under him. His back slammed into the hardwood floor and all the air was pushed out of his lungs.

"Prints!" Carly shouted. "Get off of him. Right now!"

The dog enthusiastically covered Dev's face with sloppy canine kisses.

By the time Carly got to her feet, Dev had pried Prints off his chest and set him aside. She grabbed the dog by his collar. "Sit, boy," she ordered.

The dog sat, and Carly let go of his collar.

"Sorry, Dev. When Prints sees someone lying on the floor, he thinks it's an invitation to play."

Dev got himself to the sofa and looked up at Carly. "Did you want something, Carly?"

"Want something?" She seemed to have forgotten momentarily her reason for returning. "Oh, yes." She walked around the coffee table and sat next to him on the sofa. "It's about your art. I know a dealer in Milwaukee who I think would be really interested in it. Her name is Janine Maxwell."

Dev sat back into the corner of the couch. "An art dealer?" He shook his head. "I don't think so. I'm not ready to show my stuff to anyone. Besides, it's not good enough to sell. I just paint because I can't walk yet."

Carly pushed her hand against his leg and drew it back. "Don't be so modest. I think your work is wonderful. You're very talented."

He cocked his head and sent her a sly grin. "But you don't know anything about art, remember?"

She conceded his point. "True, but Janine knows everything about it, and she's no rookie to criticism. Believe me, if she thinks your art isn't good enough, she'll let you know—vigorously."

His reluctance began to give way. He shifted closer to her. "She really knows what she's talking about?"

Carly assured him with a nod. "If your work is salable, Janine'll want it. She doesn't mind making a living. And Dev . . ." She reached toward him and laid her hand on his thigh. ". . . your talent isn't temporary like your inability to walk. In fact, exercising your art skills will strengthen them the same way working your muscles strengthens your legs."

He looked at the hand warming his thigh, covered it with his, then moved closer to her. He glanced at her and tilted his head. He didn't believe a word she said, but he was close to her again. That's all that mattered. "You sound pretty sure of yourself."

"I am," she said, nodding and tugging her hand away from him. Abruptly, she bounced to her feet and walked around the coffee table. "I'll call Janine and have her contact you."

Dev stood and struggled to keep his balance. She'd steered him toward capable people with Meka and Cammie. Maybe she knew what she was talking about with this art dealer too. "I guess it wouldn't hurt to talk to her."

Carly called Prints and walked to the front door. "You don't have anything to lose."

He forced himself to cover her steps, then leaned into the wall next to the front door. He wanted to touch her one more time before she left. He lifted his hand.

She opened the door and smiled up at him. "Good luck."

He dropped his hand and returned her grin. "Thanks."

She and Prints bounded over the porch, down the ramp, and over his property to hers. When the two of them went inside, Dev moved to the chair on his porch and sat.

As Carly disappeared, his common sense began to return. An art dealer? He must be out of his mind. His work wasn't good enough to sell, and he didn't need to be humiliated by some woman who, for all he knew, might not know a painting from a Sasquatch.

He knew taking an interest in his neighbor would upset his concentration. A few weeks ago, he thought it would be worth the distraction. Now, with one flutter of those irresistible eyes, she had him agreeing to see one of the last people on earth he'd ever attempt to meet. An art dealer.

Painting wasn't real work, it was only a distraction from his disability. He couldn't consider earning a living from the seat of his pants like it was real work. He just couldn't.

The accident might have weakened his body and forced him into a sitting position, but a woman was undermining his resolve. He needed to get back to work, his real work, welding and bolting steel, building structures of strength.

Dev popped up from his chair and maneuvered into the house. Inside the closed door he took two steps and went down. He'd overdone his time on his feet, worn himself out. He crawled back to the studio and got into his wheelchair. He twisted into a comfortable position and heaved a giant sigh of release. He stared at the canvas on his easel.

Art isn't work. It's a curse, a need, an obsession. It's complicated, demanding, sadistic, taunting. He knocked the work in progress from its perch and condemned its hold over him.

As his eyes followed the canvas' descent to the floor, they caught sight of another work he'd hidden behind a unit of shelves. He wheeled toward it and picked it up. He moved back to the easel and placed the painting on it carefully.

It still wasn't right. He hadn't yet caught her essence. Maybe he never would. Each time he saw her, he learned more about her—and he didn't always like what he discovered. She had a power over him, even though he was sure she was completely unaware of it.

He reached out his arm, ready to send the portrait of Carly to the floor with the canvas he'd knocked over a few minutes before. Instead, he caressed the cheek of the woman in the painting as though it were the real skin of the woman who had perplexed and changed him. Then he took a brush and stroked her with all the tenderness he held in his heart.

"Prints," Carly said, pouring his food into his dish, "things couldn't have worked out better. Now I don't have to find a woman to distract Dev. His art can keep him out of that workshop." She set the bag of food aside and patted the dog's head while he ate. "If he's as good as I think he is, Janine will have him in his studio night and day. She'll keep him busy enough to make them both a fortune." She fluffed Prints' fur. "But Dev is right. I don't know art, and I could be wrong."

She straightened up and walked to the kitchen window. She leaned over the sink and stared at Dev's house. "But I don't think so. There's something special, deep and passionate about his work. I can feel it like I can feel heat from a flame."

This time, the pain in her midsection didn't occur when she thought about sending Janine to see Dev as it had when she'd thought about Meka and Cammie. Maybe it did make a difference to her whether Dev had a woman of his own or not. She'd sworn off relationships for herself so she wouldn't be pulled away from her work, but Dev made her think about what she might be missing. No man had ever done that before.

Maybe she wasn't disappointed that he hadn't taken up with the ladies she'd tried to tempt him with. She might even be glad her love trap hadn't worked.

Carly shook her head and glanced at her dog. "I'm crazy, Prints."

The dog's concentration on his kibble didn't waver.

"I'm crazy," she said, turning back to look out the window in Dev's direction, "but when I'm finished with the Montgomery proposal . . ." She reached her hand toward his house and touched the glass. ". . . perhaps I should see if Dev and I have a chance."

Chapter Nine

Janine Maxwell walked from her car to the ramp that led to Devin Serrano's porch. He'd heard her drive up while he was in his studio trying to arrange his paintings. He went immediately to the living room window and peered out to see the woman who'd come to inspect his work.

As Janine moved enthusiastically along the ramp, she smoothed her hands over her light blue suit. She slung a small red purse over her shoulder and combed the fingers of one hand through her short, soft auburn curls. When she reached the porch, she pulled off her sunglasses and knocked at the door.

Dev wheeled to the entrance and opened the door.

Janine lowered her olive green eyes to Dev and flashed a vibrant smile. "Devin Serrano?" she said, scratching one finger into a curl on her tilted head.

"Come in," Dev replied, opening the door wide for her.

She stepped inside and ran curious eyes over the

layout of his living room. She bent an index finger and pressed it against her nose, then looked down at Dev. She held out her small hand. "I'm Janine Maxwell."

Dev shook her hand. "You're right on time, Ms. Maxwell."

She pulled her hand back and glanced around the room again. "Janine, please, Devin. I don't believe in formalities." She looked back at him. "Not with people I hope to be friends with," she added, smiling and winking at him. She rubbed her hands together resolutely. "I hope you don't mind, but I'm dying to see your work, Devin."

He pressed his elbows into the arms of his chair. "It's Dev, and, no, I don't mind." He wheeled toward his studio. "Right this way, Ms—Janine." When he reached the doorway, he stepped out of his chair.

Surprise covered Janine's face, and her eyes bounced up at the man towering over her. "My goodness," she said, pressing her hand to her heart, "I certainly didn't expect you to rise from your chair, especially not so ably."

"I'm recovering from an accident."

"I see," she said, trying to cover her shock. "Carly hadn't really told me anything about you except that I'd be very interested in your work. So when I saw the ramp and you in the chair . . ."

"Yes, never mind," he said impatiently as he held out his right hand to the studio. He slid his left hand to the small of her back. "Shall we?"

Janine looked up at him with indiscreet olive eyes. "My goodness," she said, winking and smiling, "you're a tall one."

Dev looked away from her and pressed against her

lower back until she moved into the room. "I don't know where you'd like to start. I've hung most of my stuff on the walls." He waved his hand around the room, then left her to sit on the table in the middle of the studio.

Janine pulled a pair of round, gold wire-framed glasses from her purse and put them on as she looked at the first painting. "Mmm," she said, inspecting his work. She moved on to the next one. "My goodness." As she studied the paintings, she slid a single finger into her curls and scratched her scalp lightly.

Dev sat back a little farther on the table and folded his arms. This was torture. He felt like he was taking a shower outside in the middle of a campground with a hundred onlookers checking him out.

She inspected two more works without comment. Again she poked a finger inside her auburn curls and scratched her head.

She stepped to the next painting, but, before she began her examination, she glanced at Dev with a wink and a smile.

He unfolded his arms and pressed his hands into the table. He lifted himself up and adjusted his position. Agony, pure agony, and it was all Carly's fault. Those vexing eyes of hers had gotten him into this position. He never should have agreed to see Janine Maxwell.

The art dealer surveyed the remaining work rather quickly, giving Dev two more winks and smiles as she moved from project to project. When she'd finished her review, she turned to Dev. She took off her glasses and bit on the end of one of the bows. She narrowed her eyes at him a long moment, then gave him another wink. "I like what I see."

Dev was stunned, but he didn't want to expose his feelings. "Meaning?" he said, raising a brow and pretending to be only half interested in what she had to say.

"Meaning?" she chuckled, and winked again. She put her finger to her scalp once more, then withdrew it. "I mean I'd like to put your work in my gallery— if it makes it that far."

He slid to the edge of the table. "Makes it that far?"

She reached toward him and laid her hand on his arm. "Yes. I have several people in mind who I'm quite sure will jump at the chance to own a few of these pieces. They could well buy up some of your art before I have a chance to put it on display."

"You're serious?" He didn't need a mirror to know his eyes were straining against their sockets, and he wasn't interested any longer in trying to hide his reaction. "You think my work is . . ." He ran the back of his hand over his mouth, then pressed its knuckles into the table. ". . . good enough?" he said, finishing his question.

Janine reached for his arm again, smiling and winking at him. "Darlin', I wouldn't be surprised if I could sell out your whole collection in six weeks."

He sprang from the table and wobbled as his weight landed on his still-recovering legs.

Janine grabbed his arms. "Steady, big guy." She pulled away and folded her arms.

"Six weeks? Frankly, I'd have been surprised if you said you could sell anything of mine in six years."

She blinked. "In six years we can both make a fortune from your talent, Dev." She glanced around at his paintings. "You've got something unique here. Your perspective is original, your message timeless, your images compelling, your technique rugged. You've captured life from a strong man's point of view. Your paintings are vigorous, but they wield a warmth that touches the heart."

He looked at a few of his works. "You see all that?"

She reached up and touched his cheek, turning his face back to her. "And more," she said softly.

Dev smiled down at her, trying to cover the disbelief he was sure must be exuding from his face. "I just paint. I didn't mean to . . ."

She boldly moved her head from side to side. "No, don't say it. Don't try to analyze it. Just do it. Paint, Dev. Paint." She reached up with both her hands and took his face. "You're an artist. Give in to the talent, and let it take you along its path. I want all the work you can give me."

He took hold of her wrists and lowered her arms, staring into her eyes. "You want more than this?" he asked, waving his arm around the room.

She stepped back and blinked at him. "Lots more," she said, scratching one finger through her curls. "I want you at that easel night and day." She opened her purse and pulled out a card, then glanced up at him. "Have you got Internet?"

He nodded crookedly.

"Good, then you don't even have to leave the house. Here is the address of a website that can send you all the art supplies you could possibly need."

"But I don't know about—"

"No," she said, covering his mouth with her hand. "I know. You're a painter. Paint. Forget everything else."

He sat back on the edge of the table. Rubbing his hand over his scratchy face, he shook his head. "This is going a little fast for me. I'm an iron worker. I only started painting because I was stuck in the chair. I'm no artist, I'm just a guy with some paints and some brushes." He stood and shook his head as he took two steps along the side of the table away from Janine. He looked back at her and sat again on the edge of the light maple wood. "I'll have to think about this, Ms. Maxwell."

Janine moved toward him. She edged alongside him on the table. "Not Ms. Maxwell," she said, reaching her fingers to his cheek, "Janine." She gently stroked his five o'clock shadow and made him look her in the eyes. "Friends, remember?" She pulled her hand from his face. Her gaze remained locked on his. Her fingers slid over his shoulder and down his arm until they rested on his iron biceps. "Dev, you're a strong man. Competence exudes from you. Whatever reason you had for starting to paint, you're going to need an even more powerful one for stopping. Your work gives you away. It tells me that you're no quitter." She massaged her fingers into his biceps, then ran them down the length of his arm until she caught his hand and held it. "There isn't an ounce, no, not a gram of weakness in you. You have talent, and you should celebrate it."

He looked away and stood, tugging his hand away from hers. He folded his arms over his chest. "You don't understand. I'm not afraid, I'm just not ready. I need time to think. You're telling me I'm something I never believed I was. That takes some getting used to."

Janine stood away from the table and gave him another wink and a smile. "This," she said, bobbing her hand from one painting to another around the room, "informs me you're more than ready. You have talent, Dev. The world deserves to see it."

"But no one knows about this except a few people." He looked toward the window, then back at her. "My friends are iron workers, Janine, men who defy physics and scoff at heights. I'm one of those men. That is who I am, who I really am."

She shook her head and curled up the corners of her mouth as she stepped near him. "Dev, remember the clients I mentioned who I'm sure would be interested in buying some of your work immediately?"

He nodded.

"One of them works on a railroad crew. Another is a truck driver." She touched his forearm, then drew her hand back. "Both of these guys are as virile as they come, but they love art. The truck driver once told me he'd give an arm and an eye to be able to paint half as well as most of my artists. But," she said, nodding crookedly, "I do get your point, and I have a way to remedy your reluctance."

He moved to the table again and leaned against it. "I'm listening," he said, running his hand over his firm jaw.

"No one has to know the work is yours but us." She turned and looked at the painting nearest her on the wall. "Here's your answer right here," she said, pointing.

Dev stepped next to her. "My signature?"

"D'Sarran. No one has to know this painting was done by Devin Sarrano unless you want to tell them. You can be known only by D'Sarran." She turned and looked up at him. "Would that ease your mind?"

Dev lifted his hand to his chin and placed a finger over his mouth. He stared at the signature he'd invented with his first finished work and slowly moved his head up and down. "An alias. Yes. Why not?"

"Do we have a deal then?"

He returned his gaze to the olive green eyes at his side and cocked his head. What did he have to lose? "Let's give it a shot."

Janine threw her arms around his neck and pulled him down low enough for her to kiss his cheek. "You're going to be glad you did this, Dev."

When she let him go, he reached for the nearby wall to steady his wobbly legs. "I hope so," he said, a bit of skepticism seeping through his voice.

She began plucking paintings from his walls. "Believe me, you won't regret getting involved with me. I'm going to make you, D'Sarran, that is, famous and sought after." Soon she had five canvasses piled in her arms. "I'll start with these."

Before he could respond, she walked out of his studio and toward his front door. He moved as quickly to the doorway of the studio as he could. "Janine, wait. We haven't discussed any of the specifics of the deal, contracts and such."

She spun around. "Yes, of course." She stepped to the coffee table and laid the paintings down. "Do you have a lawyer? I'd be happy to send the contract to him directly."

Dev nodded carefully as he seated himself in his wheelchair. "In Milwaukee, Luca Atkins. His office is on Thirty-fifth street, I think."

"Luca. Sure. I've seen him once or twice in the

gallery. Nice-looking man, tall, slender, very charming smile. Quite competent from what I've heard."

Luca's charm seldom passed by an attractive woman unnoticed, and his eye always admired beauty. Though Janine wasn't the kind of woman Dev would ever be romantically interested in, he was sure Luca would find the energy and enthusiasm tucked inside that petite, shapely package of hers very attractive. "Very competent."

Janine removed the purse from her shoulder and handed it to Dev. "You hunt down one of your attorney's cards and stick it in my purse." She picked up Dev's paintings. "I'll take these out to my car, then I'll come back for my purse."

Dev took her little red handbag and watched her small frame carry out five finished canvases. When she'd made it safely out the door, he went to a desk at the other end of his living room and took out one of Luca's cards. He slipped it into Janine's purse, then wheeled out to the porch to wait for her.

"Thanks for calling me, Malena," Carly said as the two of them strolled up the street. "I needed to get away from my work for a while. It's starting to feel like it's closing in on me."

"I know that feeling." Malena stopped walking and tugged at Carly's arm. "You know, cuz, I'm really glad we live in the same neighborhood. I like having you around. It's nice on a day like this to just call you up and say, 'Hey, Carly. Come on over, and we'll go for a walk.' "

"I like it too." Carly started to walk again. "So, how is the husband hunting coming?" She hadn't asked

Malena in at least ten days if she had any new prospects.

"Didn't I tell you about my two newest possibilities?" she asked, stepping in pace with Carly.

"No. Did you meet a couple of new guys?"

Malena bent her head from shoulder to shoulder. "One I've met, the other I saw a few nights ago at a restaurant. The restaurant man I'm having checked out. Molly, one of the waitresses there, is getting the scoop on him for me."

Carly reached up and pulled a leaf off a huge oak tree as they walked along the sidewalk. "What about the man you met? Is he a viable prospect?"

Malena pulled her lips to one side of her mouth and wrinkled her nose. "I thought so at first. He moved in across the street and two doors down last week. Playing the good neighbor, I went to introduce myself the day after the movers left."

Carly chuckled. "You didn't waste any time."

"No way," Malena said, her eyes expressing her urgency in finding a mate. "Benjamin Leon is one of the most outstanding-looking men I've ever seen, and I was sure he was under thirty."

The two continued to stroll and talk as they approached Dev's property.

"Sounds perfect so far," Carly commented.

Malena nodded. "I thought so too. Then I met him. The first thing he asked when he learned which house was mine was why did I paint it that hideous shade of green."

Carly threw her head back and laughed. "I told you to get Cammie over there and change the color as soon as you moved in. Now it looks like your hesitance may have cost you a husband."

Malena shrugged nonchalantly. "I doubt it. I don't care how good looking a man is, if he's going to fly off the handle that easily, I'm better off without him." She took a few silent steps. "But there is something about him, Carly. Even while he went on about how awful my house looked, saying how he'd seen enough olive drab in the army and all, I couldn't take my eyes off the fire in his. His gaze was blazing with passion, and I couldn't help but wonder—"

"Never mind," Carly said, putting a hand up to Malena's mouth. "I get the general idea."

"And that spice scent of his—"

Carly stopped short. "What?"

Malena looked at her, then her eyes shifted over Carly's shoulder. "Look," she said, pointing. "It's Dev."

Carly spun around and caught sight of Dev on his front porch. Janine Maxwell was walking up the ramp toward him.

"Who's the knockout coming to see him?"

Carly stared at the art dealer. "Janine Maxwell." Malena was right. Janine was a beautiful woman. She'd forgotten just how attractive the petite redhead was.

Malena smiled suspiciously at her cousin. "Another of your attempts to partner up your neighbor with someone who'll keep him out of his garage?"

Carly didn't look at Malena. "Something like that." She couldn't take her eyes off the two people now on Dev's porch.

Dev handed a red handbag to Janine. She said something to him, then leaned over to give him a hug and a kiss on the cheek.

"Looks like your plan is working," Malena said, nudging her cousin.

Carly turned vicious eyes on her and firmed her jaw.

Malena wrinkled her brows. "Or is it?" She stared into Carly's hard gaze until her cousin moved her eyes back to Dev's porch. "Seeing him with her bothers you, Carly. Why?"

Carly watched Janine get into her car and back out of the driveway.

When Janine's car pulled next to Carly and Malena, she rolled down the window and looked up at Carly. "He's wonderful, Carly, absolutely wonderful. I'll never be able to thank you enough for telling me about him." She quickly glanced behind her. "I've got to go. Thanks again."

"Sure," Carly said. She watched Janine drive away.

Suddenly Malena grabbed Carly's arm and started ushering her toward Dev's house. "Let's go say hi."

Carly pulled at her captured arm. "I need to get back to work, Malena. You go by yourself."

Malena wouldn't release her cousin's arm. "Don't be silly. It only takes a minute to say hello."

The next thing Carly knew, she was standing alongside Dev's porch, looking up at Dev, who now stood at the railing, and Malena had issued the fastest greeting and exit she'd ever seen.

Chapter Ten

Carly couldn't believe Malena had brought her to Dev and just left her alone with him. What had gotten into her usually forthright cousin?

"Hello," Dev said, peering down at her from the porch.

The sound of his voice tingled her spine. "Hi," she replied, tilting her head. "It's kinda warm today, isn't it."

"Kinda." He tilted his head. "Would you like to come up and join me on the porch? I could make us some iced tea or coffee."

No coffee, Carly thought, remembering the first and last time she joined Dev in his kitchen while he made coffee. "It's too hot for coffee. Besides," she said, inclining her head toward her house, "I've got to get back to work. I'm coming back from a walk with Malena."

Suddenly, he lifted one leg over the railing and dragged the other behind it. Then he lowered himself to the ground. He walked over to Carly and took hold of the handrail attached to the ramp. "Do you always work?"

She nodded. "I like to work."

He lifted a shoulder and let it fall. "Me too, but no one should work all the time."

A bee buzzed by Carly, and she shooed it away. "I don't work all the time," she said, batting at the bee again. "I told you I just came from a walk with Malena."

He watched her swing at a second bee. "Are you sure I can't interest you in a cold drink?"

She shook her head. She'd barely answered him when three bees appeared around her face. She ducked to avoid them as she made another effort to chase them away with her hands. Stepping to the side in the commotion, she angled her foot off the edge of the sidewalk and lost her balance.

Dev reached for her and grabbed her by the arm. "Guess I'm not the only one who's noticed your lavender scent."

Her eyes shot up to his as she regained her balance. "Lavender?"

He took a deep breath. "Mmm. You can't blame the bees for being drawn to it."

She yanked her arm away from him. He was much too close. She didn't trust herself this near him. She really did have to get back to work. She couldn't afford to lose any time on the Montgomery project. The deadline was only a few weeks away. Besides, it looked like he was already getting very friendly with Janine. She took two steps back. "Thanks for the drink offer." She retreated another two steps. "Maybe another time."

"Sure," he said, grinning at her. "Any time."

Carly spun away from him and walked home. Three feet inside her front door, she plopped down into a chair and rubbed her hands over her face. Why did she reject his friendly invitation? Hadn't she just promised herself she'd consider exploring a relationship with Dev?

But she couldn't. Not now. Too much was at stake, with her career and with him as well. She already knew he was no ordinary man. If she were to test the waters with him, she'd have to be very careful not to drown.

In the next several weeks Dev divided his time between his studio and his garage. He'd seen instant success with the first few paintings Janine had taken to sell. She'd come back to get more a few days after she'd taken the first works. Those had gone nearly as quickly as the first ones.

Janine insisted Dev concentrate on painting full-time, but a man could only sit in front of an easel so long. His woodworking grounded him in things real and tangible. It provided relief from the gut-wrenching energy painting drew from the depths of him.

As he sat in his studio starting a new project late one morning after a vigorous few hours of woodworking, a barbaric knock echoed through his living room.

Dev wheeled away from his work and responded to the insistent call. He flung the door open without looking to see who stood on his stoop. Dev gazed up at the large, dark-skinned man glaring at him, arms folded and ready to pounce on him. "Henry. What are you doing here? Didn't you get my message?"

"I got it. Now I want you to get mine. Stand up."

Gladly. Dev didn't like Henry's demeanor one bit, and he certainly didn't care for his condescending tone. He bolted to his feet and steadied his wobbly legs. "If you've got something to say, say it."

"I thought so," Henry said, looking at Dev's legs. "You're not even as strong as you were three weeks ago." He poked Dev in the chest.

Dev took a shaky step backwards. "Look, Henry, I told you that you didn't need to come today. Now why don't you go home?"

Henry poked him again. "I'll leave when I'm ready. I didn't drive all the way out here from Milwaukee just to turn tail and run."

Dev took another wobbly step back when Henry poked him for a third time. He batted Henry's hand away from his chest and gritted his teeth. "I don't appreciate the way you're acting, Henry."

"I really don't care one iota what you do or don't appreciate. If you like that wheelchair so much, you can stay right where you are. Make it a permanent part of your backside. That's up to you."

"That's right," Dev replied, glowering at him. "My recovery is my business. When I want you to come by to help me with it, I'll ask."

"You are one crazy son of a gun," Henry said, shaking his head. "You were coming along so well with your recovery. Another two weeks of work the way you'd come along in June and July, and you wouldn't have even needed that chair anymore. Do you understand what I'm saying?" He stared at Dev and waited for a reply.

He didn't get one.

"I'm telling you if we'd have kept working these last three weeks as hard as you did the rest of the summer you'd be walking everywhere now, on crutches, yes, but you'd be walking. I thought you got over this reluctance to do your therapy." He lifted a hand to his face and stroked his chin. "I believe it was a young lady inhibiting your progress before."

"She had nothing to do with it," Dev said, defensively. "Not then and not now."

"What is it, then? You depressed? Bored? Lazy?"

Dev ground his hands together and gnashed his teeth. "No, none of those things."

Henry studied him carefully a few moments longer, then glanced toward his studio. He walked to the little room and looked at the new work on the easel. Then he glanced around at the empty walls.

Dev followed him and sat in the doorway.

"Where are all your paintings?" he asked, furrowing his brows.

Dev lifted a shoulder, reluctant to admit he'd been making money off his art. "I sold 'em."

Henry's face brightened as though his little boy had just scored a soccer goal. "You did? Good for you."

A smile crawled across Dev's face. "Yeah, good for me."

"Really," he said, reaching for Dev's hand, "congratulations."

Dev shook his hand. "Thanks."

Henry looked from Dev to the easel and back again as he pulled his hand away. "Is that why you've been

neglecting your physical therapy? You've been spending all your time painting?"

Dev wheeled to his canvas and stared at his work
in progress.

Henry took hold of Dev's chair and spun it around
to bring Dev's gaze back to his. He carefully eyed his
patient. "I'm close, but I haven't hit the nail on the
head yet, have I?"

Dev lifted the corners of his mouth. "You're the first
clairvoyant football player I've ever seen."

"Got nothing to do with mind reading, Picasso. It's
got everything to do with working with hurting people.
I've learned how to recognize pain. I can see you're
full of it."

Dev laughed. "I'm full of it, all right, Henry, but
it's got very little to do with pain." He stared into the
trustworthy eyes of the confidant who'd seen him
through a mountain of misery. "I'm living a lie."

Henry scrunched down to make himself more even
with Dev. "A lie? You? No way. You're too honest
for that."

Dev shook his head vigorously. "I thought so too.
Then I started selling my art. It went like bread and
milk before a snowstorm, Henry. All of a sudden, I
wasn't an iron worker anymore. I was an artist, a man
making a living sitting on my backside." He blinked
hard, then stared his friend in the eye. "That isn't who
I am."

Henry nodded carefully. "I see."

"But I like it. And I don't want to like it. Then I
wonder how long this painting ability will last. You
know I started it when I got laid up so I wouldn't go
crazy. It was a game. Now I'm hooked on it, and I'm

afraid . . ." He spun away from Henry and rolled over to the window. "I've never been afraid of anything in my life."

Henry walked next to him and leaned his back into the wall, folding his arms. "Now I know that's a lie. There aren't any of us who've never been afraid."

"I haven't—until now."

Henry gave him a comforting grin and placed a hand on his shoulder. "What are you afraid of?" he asked, drawing his hand back.

Dev looked up at him, then back out the window. "I'm afraid if I start walking again, I won't be able to paint anymore."

Henry took a deep breath. He glanced down at the wood floor and rubbed his foot over a scratch in the dark stain. "You know one thing has nothing to do with the other, partner. In your head you know that."

Dev continued to stare out the window. "I don't know anything of the kind." As he spoke, Carly came out into her yard with Prints. She was wearing another of those big soft skirts and round-necked blouses that made her the epitome of femininity.

"Dev, you've got to do some long, hard thinking. You can't just sit there and atrophy. You've got to get up out of that chair and take command."

He heard Henry's words, but he couldn't take his eyes off of the vision outside his window.

"You're a vital man. You've got to get yourself healthy again. You've got to take chances. Get back on your feet. I guarantee you have nothing to lose and everything to gain. Partner, there's no doubt about that."

Dev nodded and stared out the window. He did

want to be on his feet again. There was too much of life passing him by.

Henry stood to his full six feet two. He put his hand on Dev's shoulder. "You let me know when you want me back."

Dev glanced up at his friend, then back at Carly. "Thanks, Henry." He twisted around and looked him in the eye. "I mean that."

A mass of white teeth glistened as Henry issued one of his understanding grins. "I know you do, partner. And I expect to hear from you in a couple of days."

Dev nodded, then looked out the window once more. "Henry," he called before the physical therapist reached the front door, "come by tomorrow."

"See you at four," he replied.

Yes. Four. That was the number. Four. Four weeks. He'd give himself that much time. In four weeks he'd be invariably vertical. He'd walk the thirty yards from his front door to hers and stand next to her. He'd inhale lavender and stare into a sea of blue. If it cost him every ounce of artistic talent he had, he'd get back his ability to walk if for no other reason than to take a chance with Carly. Henry was right. He had to take command and take a chance. And he had to quit being a coward.

Only a couple of weeks remained before a submission of plans for the Montgomery project was due. Carly was wracked with anxiety. After three weeks of relative quiet in August, Dev was again putting in hours upon hours in his workshop. But Carly knew it wasn't only noise that was tying her mind in knots. She was finally having to face the fact that the Mont-

gomery project might just be more than she was ready
to handle. Maybe she didn't yet have what it took to
be viable competition in constructing a high-rise. Perhaps she'd been too arrogant or brash or just plain
impatient.

She massaged her palms over her face as she stared
at her computer screen. If only he would stop.

She threw a wadded-up piece of paper at the monitor and pushed herself back in her rolling chair. She
stalked to the kitchen and got a glass of water. She
stared out the kitchen window as she drank.

She blinked and drank and focused on the garage
emitting the offensive sounds. Why did he have to
torment her?

She wasn't questioning the noise now. The torment
she thought of came from her heart. Dev had done
exactly what she'd set him up to do. He'd taken an
interest in a woman. Janine Maxwell visited him frequently. Several times she saw the two of them leave
together and return hours later.

Her plan had worked. She set a trap for Dev, and
he fell into it. She'd gotten him a girlfriend, and she'd
gotten peace and quiet for hours at a time. But she
couldn't work in the silence when Dev was away with
Janine. Her mind was too full of imagined liaisons
between the gorgeous redhead and the handsome man
she'd hoped to have herself one day. If Dev got serious with Janine, she'd never forgive herself.

Janine's car pulled into Dev's driveway. Before she
got out, Dev came out of the garage. He wasn't in his
chair, but on crutches. Carly's heart leaped to see him
well on his way to full recovery. Then she watched

Janine exit the car and run to Dev. She threw her arms around his neck and squeezed him hard.

Carly turned her back on him. She couldn't watch anymore.

It would be quiet for a while now, and she had a project to finish.

Fall arrived the day Carly turned in her bid on the Montgomery project. It was the worst day of her life. She'd never before submitted work that she was more ashamed of. She knew she had no chance of getting the job. She'd considered not placing a plan with Montgomery at all, but she'd promised. She'd rather turn in a poor job than not keep her commitment.

Carly spent the afternoon pacing and finding busy-work to take her mind off her failure. At one point, her frustration got the better of her. She picked up a chipped plate and a cracked glass and heaved them against the kitchen wall, shattering them quite thoroughly.

Seeing what she'd done, she decided if she wanted to throw something it would be better to do it outside. She picked up a Frisbee, a tennis ball, and a baseball and called Prints. Then she walked him to the park. She threw and he fetched until it was nearly dark.

By the time they arrived home, the sun had set and the air had chilled. Carly cleaned up the mess she'd left in the kitchen, dropping the shattered glass into a large metal trash can. When she finished, she heard a pounding on her front door.

"That's all I need," she muttered under her breath. "A visitor." She passed the mirror near the front door and caught a glimpse of herself. Her hair was askew, much of it having fallen from the French knot at the back of her head. Her peasant blouse hung off one shoulder, and she had a smudge of dirt on her cheek. She wiped the smear away, then tossed her hand at her reflection. "I don't care if I am a mess," she murmured.

She swung open the door. She saw the black T-shirt first, then lifted her eyes to meet Dev's. "What are you doing here?" she asked. "Haven't you done enough damage already?"

The smile on Dev's face vanished. His brows flew up and he struggled to reply. "I beg your pardon?"

"Yes, you." She poked a finger toward him. "It's your fault. You couldn't let your neighbors have the quiet summer they deserved. No, you had to spend five months running saws and sanders and routers and drills. That selfish screeching habit of yours has ruined everything."

He took hold of her flailing arms and stepped into the foyer, letting his crutches fall on the porch. He shut the door with his foot. "Carly, calm down, and tell me what has happened."

She pulled her arms free of him and took one step back. "You've killed my project, my hopes, my dreams. You did it." She poked him in the ribs. "You and all that noise." She pelted him in the chest with one hand, then the other, then both of them. "You've cost me everything I've ever wanted."

He took hold of her wrists and held them fast. "Carly, you're not making any sense."

She glared up at him and tried to strike his chest again. "I'm making perfect sense," she said. "I spent my whole summer working on a big project that could break my career wide open. I labored night and day over the noise coming from your shop. I asked you to stop. I demanded it, but you didn't care. You thought only of yourself and your precious hobby. You didn't care one bit that your careless behavior was ruining my life."

In the dim light of the foyer, Dev's dark eyes grew wide within his stunned expression. "I had no idea. You only mentioned the noise once."

Tears started to spill from the corners of her eyes. "Oh, Dev." Suddenly, she leaned forward and collapsed into his arms. "I'm sorry."

He wrapped her tightly against him and stroked her hair, loosening it from the confinement of what remained of the French knot. Blond silk spilled around her shoulders, and he laced his fingers through it. "Looks like you've had a bad day," he said, soothing her. "You go ahead and cry."

"I'm sorry," she said again through sobs and gulps for air.

"Never mind." He brought his hands to her cheeks and swallowed them up with his palms. He wiped his thumbs under her eyes and stared down at her. "Are you all right now?"

She tried to nod. "No," she said, forcing her head up and down. "But I will be. I'm not used to failing, and today I blundered badly. It'll take a little time to recover."

He rubbed his thumbs under her eyes again. "Is there anything I can do to help?"

She closed her eyes. She couldn't look at him. Two minutes ago she was blaming him for her problems, and now he wanted to help her. She forced her lids up. She owed him eye contact. Lifting her hands to his, she took hold of them and pulled them from her face. She took a step back and folded her arms. "You must have had a reason for coming by."

"Ah, yeah," he said, pushing his hands into his jeans pockets. "But now I think I should just forget it and go home . . . unless you need a little company."

She shook her head. "I'm fine, or I will be, but you go ahead. Tell me what you wanted."

"Well," he said, shifting his weight from one foot to the other, "Meka told me you told her you were going to take a few days off."

"That's right."

"I was thinking . . ." He glanced toward the door, then back at Carly. "Let's just forget it." He stepped toward the entrance and put his hand on the doorknob.

Carly reached for his arm and tugged him back. "Don't be silly. After the way I just treated you, I think the least I can do is listen to what you have to say. Go ahead."

He looked down at her and smiled. "Okay, if you say so, but remember, you asked for it."

"I'll remember," she said, returning his smile.

He glanced at the floor and shoved his hands back into his pockets. Then he looked up at her and said, "I was wondering if you'd come with me to Memphis."

Chapter Eleven

"Memphis?" Carly closed her eyes and shook her head. When she lifted her lids again, she asked, "What are you talking about?"

"I've got a delivery to make. I hired a courier to do the job, but he had to cancel out on me." He glanced away from her and shifted from one foot to the other. Slowly, he moved his eyes back to her as he spoke. "It's over six hundred miles to Memphis." He looked away again.

"And you'd like some company?" Carly felt his uneasiness. She tried to help him say the words he was trying to say.

His eyes darted back to hers. "Company? Sure, that'd be nice, but what I'm trying to say is, I don't think I can . . ." He shifted his weight again and thrust his hands into his pockets.

She touched his arm. "You don't think you can what?"

He shook his head, then focused on her. "I'm much

better, Carly, but I don't think I can drive that far. My truck isn't rigged with special equipment like the car I've been using these last months. It's just an ordinary truck."

"Oh, I see," she said, the tone in her voice revealing her disappointment. He wasn't asking her along because he wanted to spend time with her. He'd heard she had a few free days, and he wanted her to help him do the driving. She turned away from him and took a few steps. It never occurred to her that he needed help. Wheelchair or not, Dev had always struck her as completely capable.

He followed her steps. "You don't want to do it, do you." He cleared his throat. "I don't blame you. You've just finished a big job and need some real vacation time, not a marathon run on a delivery."

Carly nodded slowly, keeping her back to him.

"That's okay. I'll see if I can get someone else."

She heard him reach for the door and open it. Suddenly, she spun around. "How long will the trip take?"

He looked back at her, his hand braced high on the door. He lifted a shoulder and let it fall. "A couple of days. It's a long drive, but we should be able to make each way in twelve hours, maybe thirteen."

Twelve hours at a time stuck in the confined quarters of a pickup truck? She and Dev. Alone for hundreds of miles and two whole days. Carly looked down and shook her head, then raised her chin and met his gaze. She stared at him a long moment, then said, "I could be ready in the morning."

"You can? You'll go with me then?"

She'd had no intention of accepting his offer. Not now that he was involved with Janine. She firmed her jaw and looked him squarely in the eye. "I said I would." She never broke a promise.

"Great," he said, reaching toward her and touching her cheek. "I'll come by for you at seven—unless that's too early."

She moved her head with a half nod and a half shake. "Seven isn't too early."

He jerked his head forward. "Good." He turned and stepped to the porch and picked up his crutches. "Good night, Carly," he said, smiling at her. "I really appreciate this."

She shrugged indifferently. "No problem. I've never been to Tennessee. I'm sure it'll be a beautiful drive."

He leaned into his crutches and held on to his smile. "I'm sure too."

As soon as she closed the door, Carly imagined what the trip would be like. Six hundred miles in a pickup truck alone with Dev, crossing who knows how many state lines, stopping to eat in restaurants, acting like real friends.

Janine Maxwell popped into her head. Dev belonged to her now. She'd seen them embracing and kissing often enough—not like lovers, really, but Dev never seemed to mind being close to Janine. And Carly would never move in on another woman's man, no matter how irresistible he was. She knew that, and she knew she couldn't drive to Memphis with Dev without risking becoming the kind of woman who did go after another's man. She just plain had no defenses against her attraction to Dev, or at least she wouldn't in such close quarters. Desire would surely overtake her as it had in the van months before.

She couldn't go. As much as she hated to back out

on her word, she'd have to break her promise. Reneging on a promise wouldn't be half as bad as giving in to her attraction to Janine's guy.

Carly shook her head and smiled at her own foolishness. She'd made a love trap for Dev, and he'd taken the bait. All the frustration and anxiety that now plagued her was her own fault. She'd have to pay the price for her own deviousness.

Prints pounced up on her, landing his front paws on her legs. He lapped at her in an attempt to plant a dog kiss on her face.

Carly pushed him away. "Whew," she said, grimacing. "What did you get into at the park?"

The dog gave a shake and stared up at her.

"You stink, boy. I'd better give you a bath." Taking the dog by the collar, she led him to the laundry tub in the basement.

As she plowed fingers full of shampoo through Prints' fur, Carly rehearsed the efforts she'd make to get out of the promise she made to Dev. Then Prints gave her a great idea.

After having a difficult time falling asleep, Dev woke too early in the morning. He felt like a heel talking Carly into coming along with him to Memphis just so he could spend some time with her. But he hadn't lied to her. He really did need to ship his cargo to Tennessee, and he knew he wasn't yet fully capable of driving there and back himself, not in only two days anyway.

He could have asked one of the guys from the union hall or maybe even Henry or Luca to help him out.

Any of them would have been glad to oblige him. But none of them were Carly.

He knew his chances with her were slim. She was all business.

A grin crept over his face as he stretched out in his bed, tugging the sheet up over his bare chest. *Not all business*, he thought, remembering their closeness in the van.

She'd claimed to regret what they'd done, and maybe she did. She wasn't a very easy person to read.

All he knew was that he wanted to do what Henry had told him to do—take command and take chances. He was a vital man with much to offer. And Carly was all woman, whether she knew it or not. He suspected perhaps she didn't know it, or she didn't want to admit it. She'd made herself into a career machine.

Or maybe she just wanted him to think of her that way because she wasn't interested in him.

Dev threw the covers back and headed for the shower. He had to forget analysis and plunge ahead. He and Carly had a long way to go. It was time to plant his feet on the path he'd chosen and coax her along the way.

A couple of hours later, Dev was showered, packed, and ready to lead Carly along a direct course. He closed up the back of his truck, laid his crutches on the floor of the backseat of the extended cab and pulled himself up into the driver's seat. He backed the late-model black pickup out of his driveway and drove the few feet to Carly's house.

When he reached her house, she came out the front door carrying a small suitcase.

He stepped out of the truck and waited for her, lean-

ing his back into the door to take his weight off his
legs. She wore a snug pair of blue jeans that hugged
her curves. A blue shirt touched with splashes of gold
was tucked in at her tiny waist. Her long hair, the same
color of gold as in her shirt, spilled over her shoulders.

Dev had always thought it was the full skirts and
round-necked blouses that made Carly the picture of
femininity, but even in jeans Carly was every inch
female, soft and round.

Her hair bounced as she walked and her hips
swayed in rhythm. Dev could watch her move like that
all day.

"Ready?" she asked, smiling at him when she
reached the truck.

"Everything's loaded and accounted for." He took
her bag. "Let's put this in the back." He took his
crutches from the rear seat and went to put her luggage
with his things.

Carly turned back toward the house and started
walking away from him.

"Do you have more?"

She swung her head around to him. "Uh-huh."

He followed her to her porch. "Let me give you a
hand."

She walked up the steps of the wooden verandah
and turned to him. "Okay. Stay there. I'll hand this to
you over the railing."

Dev waited on the sidewalk.

She lifted a green and yellow paper bag and gave
it to Dev.

He looked at what she put in his hands and raised
his brows as he lifted his eyes to hers. "Dog food?"

"Of course," she replied, as though the question in

his voice and expression were totally out of line. "Prints has got to eat too."

"Prints?" Dev's brows arched even higher. "You're bringing him along?"

Carly moved her head from side to side, her loose hair cascading around her shoulders. "Surely you don't expect me to leave him here by himself, do you?"

He hadn't thought about Prints. "You don't think he'd be all right for a couple of days?"

"Maybe he would, but I already told him he could come along." She abruptly turned and opened the front door.

"You told him . . ."

She wasn't listening. She went inside.

Dev shook his head and looked down at the bag of dog food in his hand. "She's bringing the dog," he whispered, thinking out loud. "Either she doesn't trust me, or she's overly attached to that mutt." A grin crept across his face. She probably feels she needs protection. Maybe she does. He'd used Prints to coax Carly to come to him before. It was only fair that she use the dog to keep him away.

He decided the "two's company" idea he had when he asked Carly to go to Memphis with him gave way to the "three's a crowd" cliché with Prints joining them.

Now that Carly's attentions would be occupied by her pet, his attempt at getting closer to her would be a lot more difficult. But if he couldn't compete against a cagey canine, he didn't deserve the devotion of a divine damsel like Carly.

Minutes later, the dog's supplies were resting in the back with everything else, and Prints was sitting in the back seat, bobbing his head into the front between Dev and Carly.

As he backed out of the driveway, canine and Carly beside him, his courting hopes crashing, Dev remembered his resolve to take command. He glanced from Carly to the panting dog breathing down his neck. It was too late for that now.

All the way to Rockford, Illinois from southern Wisconsin, Carly watched Dev with fascination. She tried not to be obvious about it, shifting her eyes ahead and toward the driver's side as she commented on the pretty scenery and early colors of autumn. She was sure Dev couldn't see the awe in her eyes beneath her sunglasses.

Everything about him was male. The mere presence of him made her feel all gooey and feminine inside, something she'd never experienced before with such intensity. She hated the silly side of femininity, the schoolgirl gushiness. Yet she couldn't help feeling like a lovesick teenager next to Dev.

They took Highway 51 south out of Rockford. Dev said they'd follow it all the way to the tip of Illinois. They made small talk on the road to LaSalle, and Carly tried to put her attraction to Dev aside. She wasn't succeeding. *He belongs to Janine*, she told herself.

The previous evening popped into her head. She was steaming mad at Dev then. She'd blamed him for her failure. He had made it impossible to concentrate for much of the summer. Maybe her inadequacy wasn't all her fault. His noisiness could have ruined her chances at the Montgomery project.

She launched her eyes back at him. "What were you making in the garage all summer long—besides more racket than a thousand jackhammers?"

His face jerked toward her. "I beg your pardon?"

She firmed her jaw and stiffened her spine. "I think you owe me an explanation. I'm the one who endured that ghastly disturbance. You threw all concentration out of my head and cost me my chance at winning a contract to design a high-rise apartment building in Milwaukee." She folded her arms in front of her and narrowed her gaze. "Just what did your selfish disregard for peace and quiet in the neighborhood produce? A new workbench? A tool cabinet? Maybe you were working on some fancy molding to put up around your peg board."

His jaw turned to steel, and he stared straight ahead.

"Well?" she asked impatiently.

He took a deep breath, then another one. He let the second one out slowly. He glanced at her, then nodded toward the back of the truck. "It's back there."

"What?" Her eyes darted to the topper behind them, then back at Dev. "The cargo we're hauling to Tennessee is what you were making in your garage this summer?"

He nodded and stared back at the road.

"And you had the nerve to ask me to make the trip with you, even after you knew how upset I was last night?"

He pulled onto the exit for Pontiac and steered the truck off the road to the first service station. He shut off the ignition and turned to Carly. "Would you like me to turn back?"

That sounded like a very good idea, but she wasn't

about to answer him at the moment. She glared at him instead. Then she turned to face him squarely and stiffened her spine. "I demand to know what we are taking to Tennessee."

He arched a brow and leaned back. "You demand, do you?" he said, teasing her as though she were a child with no right to ask him the question.

"Yes. I order you to tell me." She stiffened the arms folded in front of her.

He tilted his head to one side and leaned forward. He reached toward her and lifted a thick mass of hair off her shoulder and let it fall behind her.

She yanked her shoulder away from him.

He took his arm back and drew in another deep breath. "We're hauling toys to Memphis. That's what I've been working on all summer long. My sister works at an orphanage in Budapest. The children have very little to call their own. These toys will be Christmas presents for them." He turned his attention back to the truck. He started the engine. "Unless I don't get them delivered on time to make that shipment due date in three days from now." He moved his eyes back to her. "Now," he said, letting out a sigh, "do you want me to take you home, or should we press on?"

A giant knot that started in her mouth grew in her throat. Speech was impossible. Her only means of communication was the ability to wave her arm, hoping he would understand that she meant that they should continue their journey.

"Press on then?"

She nodded stiffly.

He put the truck in gear and made his way back to the highway.

Carly yanked a pillow from the back seat and stuffed it between herself and the window. She laid her head on it and closed her eyes. She'd called him selfish. The man was the most generous person she'd ever met, and she'd called him selfish. Now she was stuck in the truck with him through two more states to Memphis and all the way back to Pine Grove. If only the pillow could swallow her up, but, even if it could, it surely would spit her out. She was sure to leave a sour taste with anything or anyone she touched.

Dev glanced toward Carly from time to time as he drove down the highway. It took her a while, but eventually she fell asleep. Once he knew for sure from the rhythm of her breaths that she was safely tucked away in dreamland, he allowed himself to admire her beauty. Even a mental picture of her took his breath away. If it weren't for her temper, he'd wonder if she were ethereal.

He smiled, remembering the times she lost her temper with him. The fire in her indigo blue eyes, the outrage in her hands and arms and face. If he didn't know better, he'd swear she was as Italian as he was. Not that all Italians were hotheaded and expressive like his own family members. He didn't mind the wrath in a woman's voice if it was warranted, and Carly Ross believed her rancor was backed with reason. Like his relatives, she was merely making a point.

In fact, her anger with him delighted him on one level. She didn't hold back because he was injured. She never gave him special treatment or looked upon him as weaker than any other man. Just the opposite was true. She'd always made him feel more potent than any woman had before. Perhaps that was why he found her so hard to resist. It was his curiosity about her that was the impetus for his recovery. She was worth taking a chance for.

Dev glanced again at the woman sleeping in his truck. If he stretched his arm out, he could easily touch her, but he wasn't at all sure he could ever really reach her. Living in the same neighborhood, they each lived in their own worlds, and his was falling apart. Each day he got stronger, he spent less time on his art and more time talking to his friends about going back to Milwaukee to work.

He straddled a line between his past and his future, Milwaukee and Pine Grove, iron work and art. Which of those worlds would be fit for Carly? Maybe his dreams of having her in his life were as unreal as anything that transpired during sleep.

Guilt struck him. He shouldn't have asked her along. It *was* selfish of him.

He glanced at her again. This time he did reach toward her. He touched the silk of her hair. It was too late to change his mind now. She was with him, and she'd stay with him as long as it took to deliver his cargo and return home.

All at once, his pickup jarred and started to pull to one side. Dev took a firm grip on the wheel.

The jostling roused Carly. "What's wrong?" she asked through the stupor of sleep.

"Just a flat tire," he replied gently. "Go back to sleep. I'll fix it, and we'll be on our way."

Dev pulled off the highway to a safe space and opened the door.

Prints bound into the front seat and started to bark.

"Okay, boy," Dev told the enthusiastic dog. "You get the lug wrench, I'll get the tire."

Chapter Twelve

Prints' yelping brought Carly to full consciousness. She tossed the pillow she'd been sleeping on into the backseat and brushed her hair away from her face. Then she went out to help Dev with the tire.

"Let me help," Carly said when she saw Dev lying on the ground to get the spare from underneath the box of the pickup.

"You can get the tool box if you'd like. It's just inside the gate," Dev called from the ground below the truck.

Carly put the gate down, and Prints jumped into the truck, frolicking on the dropped metal. His vivacious movements sent the vehicle bouncing up and down.

"Prints!" Dev whistled for the dog. "Stop jolting the truck."

Carly pulled the tool box from beneath the luggage, set it on the ground next to Dev, and ordered her dog out of the truck. "Sorry, Dev. Are you all right?"

"No harm done." His deep voice echoed along the ground.

"Do you need anything else?" she asked, bending down so she could see him.

"No. I'll have this done in a jiffy." He finished releasing the tire and brought it down to the ground. He pushed it from beneath the truck, then slid out himself. When he sat up at the end of the bumper, he banged his head into the tailgate. "Son of a—" he said, cutting himself off as he rubbed a hand over his injured skull.

Carly instantly pushed the tailgate up and dropped to her knees. "Dev, I'm sorry." She took his face into her hands. "Are you all right?" She quickly planted a kiss on the injury and pulled back to look at him, still holding his face in her hands.

His dark eyes darted up to her, and a smile inched across his face. "I'm fine."

Prints didn't waste any more time joining the duo on the ground. Now that they were at his level, he was going to make the most of it. He bolted to Dev and pounced on his legs. His tongue reached for the man's cheeks.

"Prints!" Carly shouted, grabbing at her dog's collar.

The dog happily obliged what he thought was a request from his owner to become part of the play. He leaped toward her, knocking her flat on the ground.

Dev laughed and shoved the dog away from Carly as he reached for her hand. He pulled Carly to a sitting position and sternly ordered Prints to sit and stay.

The dog obeyed.

Dev leaned on the bumper and got himself to his

feet, then he pulled Carly to hers. He brushed his hands over her to clean off the sand and grass. He pulled weeds and sedge from her hair, then tucked her locks neatly over her shoulders. "There," he said, "good as new."

She tucked her shirt into her jeans, then reached to wipe a smudge from his cheek. "Sorry about Prints. He loves to attack and play whenever I'm on the floor or the ground."

Dev dusted himself off and grinned at her. "I remember," he said, eyeing her carefully. "He got us in my living room earlier this summer."

"That's right," she said, remembering the fiasco.

Dev leaned into the bumper as he made his way to the tire on the rear passenger side.

Carly repeated Dev's order to Prints and commanded him to stay.

He wagged his tail and didn't move.

She moved to the side of the truck. "Should I work the jack or loosen the bolts?"

Dev's head jerked to his left, and he caught her eyes with his. The shock in his expression told her he probably believed her incapable of doing either. He suddenly glanced at Prints, then back at her. "Why don't you use the time to take Prints for a walk. If we're both on the ground, he might come after us again. Besides, if you can wear him out, he'll be content to rest easy when we continue on."

"If you're sure you don't want some help."

He waved his arm, shooing her on her way. "Go. I'll have this taken care of in no time."

Carly called the dog and went off with him, letting him run ahead of her. She found an old tennis ball and played catch with Prints for a while some distance from Dev. Later, she shielded her eyes from the bright sunshine of midday and glanced in Dev's direction to see if he was finished with the tire.

Catching sight of him from thirty yards away, she said, "Holy smoke, Prints. He took off his shirt." She glanced up at the sun. It was a warm day, and changing a tire was hard work. He had good reason to try to make himself more comfortable, but Dev Serrano was tempting enough fully clothed. She'd never be able to handle seeing him shirtless.

Suddenly she called Prints to her, then told him to go to Dev. If he saw the dog coming, he'd know Carly was on her way. That would prompt him to replace his shirt.

Carly watched Prints bound ahead of her while she kept her eye on Dev. He was at the back of the truck now. The tailgate was down on the truck, and Dev appeared to be washing himself. He ran a rag over his arms and chest, then poured water across his neck. Next he took a towel from the back of the truck and wiped it over himself carefully.

Prints arrived at the precise moment the unsuspecting man reached for his dark T-shirt. Carly was only a few yards from the truck by then. She saw the dog sink his teeth into Dev's shirt and tug it out of his hands.

Dev instantly grabbed for the shirt.

Prints loved tug-of-war games. He locked onto the soft cotton even more determinedly. Seconds later, Dev's shirt was a tattered mess.

Dev ordered Prints to sit and drop the shirt.

Carly wanted to rush in on the scene and scold her

naughty retriever, but Dev's half-naked condition held her back.

Dev picked up the tattered fabric and said to the offensive dog, "I guess I can always use another grease rag." Then he reached into the back of the truck and pulled out his bag.

When he began to slide a clean black shirt over his head, Carly at last felt comfortable about approaching. "He did it again. Sorry, Dev."

Dev tugged his shirt over his rippled body and tucked it in at his narrow waist. He shrugged. "It's just a shirt."

Carly took hold of Prints' collar. "I'll put him inside."

Dev nodded toward her, then put his bag away.

Carly stuffed the dog into the backseat. She went to help Dev put the rest of the tools and the flat tire away. She glanced around the corner of the truck before she rounded it. What she saw broke her heart. Dev could hardly move.

She inched closer to him. "Can I help with anything?"

He craned his neck toward her and tried to hide the grimace of pain on his face. "I can manage. You look after the dog." He lifted the tire into the back of the truck, and Carly feared he'd pass out from the agony the movement caused him. He leaned into the tailgate and looked at her, panting, his dark eyes burning. "Would you mind driving for a while?"

She nodded. "Sure. That's why I'm here."

His breaths heaved in and out as he moved his head up and down. "Good. Go start the truck and crank up the air conditioning. I'll join you in a minute."

Carly did as he said. While she waited, she reached into the little cooler and took out a cold drink for Dev. She put it in the cup holder. Then she poured water from a gallon jug into a dish for Prints to drink.

Momentarily, Dev opened the door and dragged his body into the cab.

Carly gave him the cold soda, and he drank heartily.

She put the truck in gear and maneuvered back onto the highway. They were south of Decatur now near Pana.

As she steered the pickup down the highway, Carly often glanced toward Dev.

He twisted and moved. It was easy to see he couldn't get comfortable.

She couldn't stand to see him suffer. She should have insisted on helping him with the tire. Regret was useless. She needed to do something to take his mind off his pain.

"Dev," she said quietly, "tell me what it's like to be an iron worker."

He was leaning his head into his right hand, his elbow pressed into the door near the window. He turned to her. "Why would you want to know about that?"

She stared straight ahead and shrugged. "Maybe I just want to know what it's like to walk on steel high above the ground. I can barely imagine what it might be like, much less ever get the chance to do it."

"Sometimes it's scary, but most of the time it's exhilarating. It gives a sense of power, which can be very dangerous. An iron worker has to learn to ignore that feeling of invincibility and remember just how vulnerable he really is. A sudden gust of wind, a missed step, a bout of clumsiness, and he's history." He shifted in his seat again. "It isn't the kind of work just anyone can do." He stopped talking a moment, then he said, "Your work is that way too. It takes special skills to be an engineer."

She glanced at him, then back at the highway. "I suppose so."

"You told me the day we went fishing that you did a lot of consulting on small projects. Do you like that kind of work?"

"I love it, but I'd really like to get into doing high-rises. You know, build a reputation good enough to have jobs seeking me instead of me seeking them."

"Don't you get enough offers on the smaller projects?"

"Actually, right now, I've got more than I can handle. Business really picked up this summer."

He adjusted his position again. "I've worked on lots of different construction projects, from a two-story retail store to a fifty-story office building. You know what I found?"

She glanced at him and grinned. "What?"

"I discovered the smaller projects are the most fun. They don't take long to finish, so I get a sense of completion with them much sooner than with a skyscraper that can take years to complete."

Carly stared at the road and nodded. "That's true. It is nice to see a project done in only a few months or even weeks. The most fun is the beginning and the ending. The middle is only the long part between the fun parts."

"Exactly," he said, twisting himself once more.

She glanced at him again and caught him staring at her. "What?" she said, wiping a hand over her cheek as though he'd been eyeing a smudge.

"I was just thinking. You enjoy doing small projects. You've already got a good reputation built with the smaller jobs. Carly, you've already achieved your goal. Jobs are seeking you out. Just because they aren't for the construction of major factories or hospitals or twenty-story office buildings doesn't diminish their importance. Why not stick with the fun stuff and enjoy your job instead of knocking yourself out running after work that won't be as pleasurable?"

Carly ignored his observation. "Look," she said, pointing. "I meant to stop to get something to eat at Pana, but I didn't. We should be able to find something in Vandalia. Do you want to stop?"

Dev saw the sign she pointed to and agreed they should have lunch. "Carly," he said, "think about what I said."

She turned onto the business district. "Pancakes, sandwiches, soup, or pizza?"

She saw Dev grin from the corner of her eye. "Anything," he replied. "Suddenly, I'm starving."

It was nearly ten when they arrived in Memphis. Dev made arrangements to deliver the toys early the next morning so they could turn around and go straight back to Pine Grove.

Dev took Carly to a very nice hotel and ordered suites for both of them. He showered and sat in the hot tub in his room to soothe his aching muscles. The hot, swirling waters invigorated him. He dressed in clean jeans and a fresh T-shirt, grabbed his crutches, and went out to get a dose of night air. He walked slowly through the courtyard of the hotel and headed for the man-made pond. Down by the water he found a bench. He laid his crutches alongside it and lowered himself to the wooden seat. He let out a deep breath, laced his fingers behind his head, and stared at the moon's reflection in the water.

His insides were shaking from the events of the day. Being near Carly had kept him on edge, but when he had to change that flat tire, he'd nearly blacked out.

The smell of the rubber, the feel of the lug wrench in his hands, the pump of the jack, all of it was a reminder. It had been a year since he'd last changed a tire, a year of agonizing recovery after he was hit while he played good Samaritan to a stranded woman.

When he worked on his own pickup, it all came back to him. Several times while he worked he doubted his ability to finish the job. But he did finish it, and he would again if it ever became necessary. And if another woman needed his help, he'd give it just as he had then.

The accident was over. He was nearing the completion of his recovery. Soon he would be as strong as ever.

He inhaled the sweet night air deeply and closed his eyes. He sat in the quiet and let his mind rest. He breathed in and out slowly and deliberately.

The sweetness of the air suddenly grew sweeter still, and Dev immediately knew the scent that tingled his senses. He opened his eyes and smiled up at her. "Please," he said, waving his arm across the bench beside him, "sit down."

Carly sat a few feet away from him. "You're sure I'm not disturbing you?"

"Not at all." He could have sworn he actually heard his heart sing. He'd never needed Carly's company more than he did at that moment, when he was so full of self-doubt and sad memories. "I'm glad to have the company."

"Good." She looked at the lake and kept her eyes focused there. "I wanted to thank you for what you said about my work. You were right."

He stared at the shine in her eyes. It was too dark to see exactly what color they were now, but he didn't care. She was there near him, and nothing else mattered. He reached toward her, straining to touch her, then drew his arm back. "About what?"

She looked up at him, her eyes reflecting enough light to tell him that they were midway between sea blue and indigo. "I have reached my goal. I am being sought out, and," she said, raising her hand to her forehead and shaking her head, "if I haven't lost anyone by putting them off to work on my 'dream project,' then I should stay on track to further success." She flashed a smile up at him, then moved her eyes back to the shimmering water.

Dev slid a few inches closer to her without her noticing. He laid his arm along the back of the bench, and lifted a lock of her hair from her shoulder. "Carly, I am sorry my work in the shop bothered you so much. If I had anything to do with you losing your project—"

"No," she said, spinning toward him and raising her hand in front of his mouth. "What you said today made me realize that the fact that I did such a terrible job on the Montgomery project was all my own fault.

Noise or not, I bit off more than I could chew. I think deep down inside, I really didn't want to give up my small projects to be consumed by a big one." She pulled her hand back to her lap. "You helped me realize that today too." She took a deep breath and let it out slowly. "There's nothing wrong with making a living on small engineering projects, especially when those make me so happy."

He touched her hair again and looked into her eyes until she turned them away.

"Dev," she said, gazing at the lake.

"Yes?"

She looked back at him. "What's wrong? Something's troubling you. I can tell."

The last thing he wanted was to share his afternoon cowardice with her. It was bad enough that he knew about it. "Nothing important."

Keeping her eyes locked on him, she inched a little closer. "I'd love to help, if I can. It's the least I can do after I spent so much time blaming you for my shortcomings. And, besides," she said, tilting her chin, "you helped me see things more clearly about my career. I owe you."

He shook his head without letting go of her eyes. His fingers trailed through the ends of her hair. "You don't owe me a thing."

"Please?"

He hadn't seen that look before. It grabbed him by the throat and forced words from his mouth. "The last time I changed a tire was the night of my accident. I thought about it today when I fixed the flat on the truck."

Her lower lip quivered, and she reached her hand

toward his cheek. She pulled her hand back and shook
her head. "Don't think about the awful accident, remember the generous spirit you showed in helping the
stranded lady. It's the same spirit that moved you to
give dozens of nameless children a little treasure for
Christmas."

He didn't feel generous, not when she gaped at him
with those magnetic eyes or while her exciting scent
clouded his senses. He felt only selfishness. He wanted
her. And he couldn't wait any longer.

As he moved next to her, he laced his fingers
through her hair. When he was close enough, he
cupped the back of her head and tilted her face up to
his. He stared into her soul and traced the line of her
face with his free hand. He smiled at her, drinking in
her beauty. He touched his finger to her lips, then
leaned to kiss what he'd touched.

She tasted sweeter than she smelled, and she felt
softer against him than what was legal. As he sat in
the moonlight holding her next to his heart, he closed
his eyes. As long as his lids were down, this dream,
if that was what it was, would be real.

But he couldn't resist another look at her face or
her eyes or her nose or her ears, at all of her.

He dragged his fingers from her hair and stared
down at her. Slowly he slid his hands along the length
of her arms, making sure she was real.

When he reached her fingers, he lifted them to his
mouth and tasted each of them. He turned her hands
over and pressed his lips to her palms.

Carly let out a sigh that penetrated him while he
kissed the insides of her hands. "Dev," she whispered.

He had to have her back. Now. He pulled her into

his arms and took the lips she willingly offered to him. Dear heaven, she was so giving, so trusting, so enticing. He boldly took more.

He slid his hands back up her arms and took possession of her head and held her firmly as he kissed her even more deeply. More, his heart cried. All of her.

Cupping one hand at the back of her head, he moved the other to her back, slowly moving it to her waist. He gently rubbed his fingers across the small of her back and pressed her even closer.

The sudden movement of her tighter against his chest forced a small cry from her depths.

The wanton sound urged him on. He lifted her onto his lap and kissed her with his whole body and soul. He heard her whimper and felt her wrap her arms around him, squeezing him with all of her feminine strength.

"Dev," she said in a ragged breath when his lips traveled to her throat. "What's happening to us?" Her words had barely left her mouth when her lips sought and devoured his.

Suddenly, Dev pulled away. He stared down into Carly's dark eyes, drugged with desire. She was his for the taking, vulnerable and trusting all at the same time.

Dev slid her off his lap and put distance between them.

"What's wrong?" she asked, mystified by his sudden rejection.

Guilt tore at Dev's insides, and he began to feel sick. It wasn't enough that he'd tricked her into coming on the trip with him, now he was seducing her, and it was working. He was despicable. "It's getting late," he whispered.

"But, Dev," she said barely loud enough for him to hear.

He couldn't look at her anymore. If he spent only two more seconds losing himself in those eyes, he'd scoop her into his arms and carry her back to his suite, injured legs or not. "Good night, Carly," he said, standing. "I'll see you in the morning."

"Dev, wait." She reached toward him and covered his arm with her hand.

He took her hand from his arm and picked up his crutches. He looked down at her one more time. He leaned to give her a quick kiss on the cheek and fled back to his room.

Chapter Thirteen

In rare moments of sleep during the night, Carly dreamed of Dev. Now, early in the morning, her thoughts of him were even more intense.

She pulled herself up in bed and stacked pillows behind her. She glanced toward the bathroom and saw Prints sound asleep in front of the door. It would probably be quiet for a while.

She leaned into the soft pillows at her back and let out a deep breath. The happiest moments of her life had taken place the night before. Dev, moonlight, shimmering water, pure romance. The ravenous look in his eyes, tender caresses along her arms, his strong fingers dragging through her hair, then holding her fast while he devoured her with potent kisses—he'd taken over her will, and she'd have given him anything he wanted.

But he didn't want her. Surely, he knew she was his for the taking. He had to be aware she had no defense against him. She lay completely open to him, vulnerable, willing, hoping he wouldn't let her go. But he didn't want her.

He'd made her drunk with desire, stationed her at the edge of starvation for him and placed her within reach of a passionate pleasure she desperately wanted to discover. Then he ripped it all away from her without any explanation at all.

Only two things could make a man walk away from what they shared last night. He'd gotten carried away by a moment, then realized he was with a woman he had no real interest in, or he was already involved with another woman. Janine Maxwell. It had to be his interest in her. He must indeed be committed to her. Who could blame him? She was gorgeous and full of life. She wasn't a dull old engineer who crabbed at him and blamed him unfairly.

Carly tugged the covers up to her chin. "If I don't make it as an engineer," she mused, "I suspect I could have a career as a matchmaker." She'd certainly found someone for Dev.

How she wished she hadn't.

She took a deep breath. She had to forget Dev and concentrate on other things, like her career. Dev was right about sticking with the smaller projects. Life would be much easier that way, and there was no better time to begin than that minute.

Carly threw back the covers, got out of bed and stepped over her dog on her way to the bathroom. She showered and dressed, then took Prints for a walk and brought him back to the room. She left him a few minutes while she went out to get a roll and coffee from the coffee shop and some office supplies from the hotel convenience store. As she sat at the table in her suite munching on a caramel roll and sipping a cafe latte, Carly begin making notes on one of the projects she intended to work at as soon as she took a few days off.

Dev interrupted her an hour later.

Carly answered his knock at her door. "Is it eight already?" She let Dev in. "Give me a minute," she said, looking around the room and panicking. "I was working and lost track of time." She quickly threw her belongings into a bag.

"Take it easy, Carly. A ten-minute delay won't hurt us." He leaned into his crutches and watched her bustle about the room. "Is there anything I can help with?"

Prints was at Dev's legs by now.

Carly glanced at him, then at the dog. "I suppose Prints could use a little more exercise before we stick him in the backseat of the truck." She picked up the leash lying on the bed and went to Prints to fasten it. When she handed the lead to Dev, he took hold of her arm.

He looked down at her, his eyes more piercing than ever. "Carly, about last night . . ."

She wanted to look away, but he wouldn't let her. "I know," she said softly.

He blinked, and she used the spell-breaking movement to release her eyes from his.

She laid her hand over the large one covering her arm, pulled it away from her, and let it fall. She stepped back and glanced up at him, then turned away. "We were both very tired. Let's just forget it and go home."

She felt him close in behind her, then scrunched her eyes shut as his warm breath caressed her neck.

"I didn't mean to—"

She spun around and pressed her fingers against his mouth. "Please, Dev, don't say anymore. It's over. We have a long drive ahead of us again today. We'll both be more comfortable if we forget last night ever happened."

When he nodded slowly, she pulled her hand away. "Whatever you say," he said softly, his voice husky.

If he didn't move back in the next half a second, she'd undo what she'd just done.

Dev stepped back.

Carly finished packing.

Dev drove north on Interstate 55 through Arkansas past Blytheville into Missouri. He continued until he met Interstate 57, followed it into Illinois and picked up U.S. Highway 51. He followed this road through most of the Land of Lincoln. As he watched the road, he glanced toward Carly. She worked intently on her designs, spreading papers all over the front seat.

Without conversation or a radio to break the monotony, Dev had too much time to think.

Regrets. He'd made a mistake asking Carly along. He executed an even bigger blunder the night before when he took her into his arms. Everything he did must have been wrong. If it weren't, she wouldn't be so cold to him now. Or maybe she was truly that career-centered.

He glanced over at her. She wore one of the soft skirts and blouses he loved on her. Her long locks clung together in an elastic at the back of her head. Stubborn curls insisting on their freedom framed her beautiful face.

No way could any woman as exquisite as Carly Ross be interested only in her job. No woman who kissed the way she did or who melded into a man the way she'd clung to him could live without passion. She was as female as they came. If she didn't want anything to do with him, it was his fault.

He hadn't treated her the way he should have. He'd been too callous or inconsiderate or clumsy. For crying out loud, he'd never even invited her on a date. This drive to Memphis, the trip he tricked her into, was the only time he'd invited her to do anything with him.

What a knothead he'd been. A woman like Carly, caught up in her work, had to be enticed with romance, flowers, candy, attentive gestures, movies and late dinners, soft music, candlelight. All he'd done was ask her to help him drive his truck, then taken advantage of her in a weak moment.

He glanced at her again as she turned another page in her notebook. He returned his eyes to the road and shook his head. It was impossible now. He couldn't get her to put her work aside if he was on fire. He'd blown the one chance he had.

Dev took a deep breath and let it out slowly. He'd lost women before, and he'd gotten over it. But he didn't care about any of them the way he did about Carly. He glanced at her one more time and drew in another long breath. He'd never feel this way again. This pain of loss was more disabling than his accident had been.

Carly drove through a good portion of Illinois on the way back to Pine Grove. She was grateful that Dev slept while she drove. The less interaction she had with him, the better. No matter what she'd said to him in her hotel suite that morning or what she'd decided about focusing her life on her career, the mere presence of Dev so close to her kept her on the edge of intimacy with him. She wanted him so much. She needed to pour her heart out to him and share everything she'd ever thought in her life. She ached for him to know how much it hurt her to be out of his embrace.

Facts were facts. It didn't matter how she felt about her neighbor. He was off-limits. He belonged to Janine.

Weeks after the trip to Memphis, Carly was fully engaged in her engineering duties. All her days were quiet now, but the silence didn't enhance her productivity. Just as when the neighborhood was noisy, some days were good, some not.

The days when work sat neglected on the drawing board or computer Carly spent looking out the window. She couldn't take her eyes off Dev's house.

She saw Janine coming and going. Sometimes Dev would drive off with her, and they'd be gone for hours at a time. Always Janine offered affectionate greetings and good-byes. It was the worst thing about living next door to Dev, watching his relationship with Janine grow.

Carly could see that Dev was getting stronger every day. She was happy about that. He deserved to be well and fully recovered. It was cruel that he'd been punished for doing a good deed.

Prints frequently wandered over to Dev's house, and once in a while she'd have to fetch the golden re-

triever. When she did, she kept her encounters with
Dev brief and the conversation superficial.

One day as Carly suffered over a lack of an idea
for a project she'd taken on, she heard a faint knock
at her front door. It was so light that she wasn't sure
anyone had knocked at all.

When she went to answer the call, she found Mr.
Cosgrove standing on her stoop with a huge bouquet
of flowers.

The old man, thin, wrinkled, and dressed in a brown
suit, smoothed a hand through the few sprigs of white
hair that covered his mostly bald head and shifted his
cocoa-colored eyes to meet Carly's. "Good afternoon,
young lady. Is Mrs. Applebee home?"

Carly put her hand over her mouth a moment then
drew it away. "She doesn't live here, Mr. Cosgrove.
She used to live over there," she said, pointing to
Dev's house. "She's gone now, remember?"

"Gone?" He lifted his thinning, white brows. His
eyes flitted from side to side, then a soft smile inched
through the antique lines of his face. "Oh, yes. I remember. She had to visit her sister in Florida. Her son
just got back from Viet Nam. He was wounded there,
you know."

Carly furrowed her brows and shook her head.
"That's a terrible shame. War is full of tragedy."

His gaze moved beyond her and a great distance
settled into his eyes. "It's bad. I know that firsthand."

Tears began to well in her eyes as she sensed the
pain in his words. "Would you like to come in and
have a cup of tea, Mr. Cosgrove?"

He looked down, then back up at her. He gave her
a half-grin and shook his head. "No, no. I couldn't do

that. If Elly isn't here, I'll go home. I think I could use a nap."

"Be careful on your walk home, now," Carly cautioned, fearing the old man might lose his footing in the wet leaves. Now that it was past the middle of October, there were more leaves on the ground than there were in the trees.

"I will," he replied, turning away from her. He took three steps toward the edge of the porch, then spun back to her. "Young lady," he said in his gravely voice, "since Elly isn't here, perhaps you'd like to have these flowers."

"Oh, I couldn't," Carly said, shaking her head.

He walked back to her and put them into her hand. "I insist. I'm allergic, so they're of no use to me."

Carly smiled and nodded toward him. "Thank you, Mr. Cosgrove."

He shook his head and returned her smile. "They pale next to you, my dear."

Carly opened her mouth to thank him once more, but Mr. Cosgrove stopped her cold.

"Oh, my goodness," he said, slamming a withered hand into his thin lips. "This is five-zero-seven. Elly lives at five-zero-nine. I have the wrong house."

She reached her hand toward him and spoke calmly. "Five-zero-seven or five-zero-nine, Mrs. Applebee is still gone, Mr. Cosgrove."

"Oh, yes." He smiled again. "Florida. To see her sister."

"Thanks for the flowers, Mr. Cosgrove."

"You're welcome, my dear."

She watched the old man wobble down the steps of her porch, then she closed the door. She went straight to the kitchen sink. She pulled a vase from the cabinet beneath it and filled the black and pink china with water. As she was arranging the flowers, pounding fists pelted the door.

She immediately stopped what she was doing and ran to answer the frantic call. She swung the door open and saw a frightened Mr. Cosgrove, panting and pointing.

"I need your bat. Quick. Get it at once." He spat the words between gulps for air. "A prowler. At Elly's."

The knot that had appeared in Carly's midsection the instant she'd seen Mr. Cosgrove disappeared as quickly as it had come. "It's all right, Mr. Cosgrove." She stepped onto the front porch and pointed at Dev standing on his own porch. "That's Devin Serrano. He lives there now."

"No! I need a bat. I left mine at home. I should have brought it with me." Horrified eyes begged her for help.

"Please, Mr. Cosgrove, you've got to calm down. I'm telling you that man," she said, pointing again at Dev, "is not a prowler. He's a neighbor. He wouldn't hurt a fly."

He shook his head forcefully. "Your bat. Get it right away."

It seemed the only way she could get him to calm down was to do what he wanted. "Okay. Just a minute."

He let out a breath and began to calm down right away.

Carly searched through the closet off the foyer. She was sure she had a baseball bat in there somewhere.

She'd kept one to use on prowlers herself. As soon as she found it, she went back to Mr. Cosgrove and handed it to him.

The old man took hold of the solid wood and tried to pull it away from her.

"Wait a minute, Mr. Cosgrove. You can have the bat, but I'm coming along with you. I want to prove to you this man is no threat."

He agreed, and she released her grip on the bat.

She helped him down the stairs and held his arm as they walked across the lawn to Dev's house.

Dev caught sight of them as they crossed his property line. A grin covered his face, and he reached a hand up to cover it. "Good afternoon, Mr. Cosgrove, Carly."

Mr. Cosgrove eyed him carefully, then looked up at Carly. "He acts as though he knows me."

Carly gave his arm a squeeze. "He does, Mr. Cosgrove." They stepped to the sidewalk in front of Dev's porch. "This is Devin Serrano. You remember him, don't you?"

The old man looked up at Dev. He shook his head. "Not sure. I need a better look." He turned to go up the ramp and nearly stumbled.

Dev leaped toward the top of the ramp. "You stay there, Mr. Cosgrove. I'll come down."

Mr. Cosgrove lifted his bat and shook it. "Okay, but don't make any sudden moves. I was in the war, you know. I know how to use a bat."

Carly marveled at how well Dev traversed the long wooden ramp he'd needed for coming and going in his wheelchair. His recovery was progressing beautifully.

Dev walked next to Mr. Cosgrove and Carly. He put his hands out in front of him. "I'm completely harmless. Remember me now?"

Cosgrove squinted his eyes and scrutinized Dev's face. "You're the guy that was in the wheelchair, aren't you?"

Dev grinned at him. "That's right."

"And now you're walking?" His gravely voice started to crack, and a tear glistened in his eye. "Not all our veterans healed up as good as that, son. I'm glad to see you did." He shook his head. "That war is a bad thing." He handed the bat back to Carly and let out a big sigh. "I'm going home now, young lady. I need to rest. You take care of this soldier. He's served his country. I'm sure he can use the love of a good woman."

Dev and Carly stood together and watched the old man tackle the last few yards between his house and Dev's.

"Poor Mr. Cosgrove," Carly said, wrapping her hands around the bat.

"I suppose he's a nice old guy, but I've never been able to tell. He's always coming after me with a bat." He touched the wood in Carly's hands. "I'm glad you finally got that thing away from him. Now I don't have to worry about running into him in the dark."

Carly swung her eyes up to meet Dev's. "Oh, this isn't Mr. Cosgrove's bat. It's mine."

"Yours!" Dev pushed his brows together. "You gave him a bat to use against me?"

"It was the only way I could get him to calm down. He thought you were a prowler."

"He could have hit me with that thing, and it would have been your fault," Dev said incredulously.

Carly laughed at the awful expression on Dev's face. "I think you'd have seen it coming, Dev. It takes him ten seconds just to lift it."

He laughed with her and agreed.

Carly bobbed her head toward her house. "I'd better get back to work."

"Already?" he asked, tilting his head and lifting his brows. "I thought we could talk awhile. I've hardly seen you since we went to Memphis."

She set the bat on the ground and held the top of it with one hand. "I've been working pretty hard."

A loud noise came from Mr. Cosgrove's house. Dev and Carly both looked in that direction.

"What do you suppose that was?" Carly asked.

Dev turned back to her. "His front door. He always slams it." He folded his arms and narrowed his eyes at her. "What was Cosgrove doing over at your house? I've never seen him go over there before."

She lifted a shoulder and let it fall. "He got mixed up. He thought my place was Mrs. Applebee's."

"You're lucky he didn't bring his bat," Dev teased.

"Actually," Carly said, tossing her hair over her shoulder, "he did bring me something."

"A catcher's mitt?"

She playfully pushed his chest. "No, of course not. He brought a lovely bouquet of carnations and roses. He got them for Mrs. Applebee, but he gave them to me."

Dev kicked at a rock that didn't belong on his sidewalk, then looked back up at Carly.

"I'll say this for the old codger. He may not be as spry as he used to be." She put her hand over her heart and sighed. "But he sure knows how to romance a sweetheart." She shook her head and stared at Mr. Cosgrove's place. "He must have loved Mrs. Applebee a whole lot."

When Carly looked at Dev again, he was staring at her as though he were seeing her in a different way. "Is something wrong?"

Dev shrugged. "Not really." He grinned at her and straightened his spine. "I guess I'm still not used to being threatened with a bat."

Carly chuckled. "I think you're safe now. So as long as you no longer need my services as a bodyguard, I'd better get back to work." She spun to leave.

Dev took hold of her arm and turned her back to him. "Carly, come inside for a while. I'd really like to talk with you."

More than anything in the world Carly wanted to forget Janine and do exactly what Dev suggested. She wanted to go into his house, talk with him, laugh with him and coax him to pin her between himself and the sink again. Only this time nothing would interrupt them. They'd play out the scene completely, and Carly would recall with great splendor the sheer delight of uniting with Dev in the world's most passionate kiss.

But she couldn't forget Janine, and she had no right to coax Dev into anything. So she told him, "Maybe another time. I need to get back to work."

He nodded and spoke softly. "Sure, Carly, go ahead."

It took more strength to turn away from him than Carly ever imagined, but she did what she had to do. She went home and got back to work.

Chapter Fourteen

By the time the second week in November came around, Dev felt as strong as he had before his accident. All the work with Henry was finally paying off. He reveled in raking leaves, was enchanted with emptying eaves, and found happiness in hanging storm windows as he prepared for the winter season. The previous November he'd been completely helpless. On a good day, he'd been able to shave and brush his teeth.

Thanksgiving would arrive soon. Last year he'd cursed the holiday. This year he'd have plenty to be thankful for.

The elm trees in the neighborhood had shed the remainder of their leaves. Some of the maples and oaks were stripped clean, others stubbornly hung onto their browns and reds and yellows. They weren't yet ready to relinquish their adornment. Dev knew how they felt about giving things up. He'd renounced nearly everything that was a measure of him before the accident, his work, rock climbing, bowling, tennis, racquetball. But his confinement brought new interests into his life. Without his injury he'd have never started to paint, he would have spent little time woodworking, and he'd have never met Carly.

Working high on a ladder replacing a few torn shingles near the edge of his roof one day, Dev reflected on the last year. It had been one of challenge and change. To his great surprise, he found himself grateful for the opportunity to have been able to brave the demands and explore talents—and meet new people.

Carly. Again. She was always on his mind. He would never forget her as long as he lived next door to her. If he thought he had a chance at all with her, he would romance her and woo her, but she'd never relinquish any time that could be spent on her career. She always had to get back to work. Yet he wasn't ready to give in to the demands of his old buddies and return to iron working.

Before he finished his shingling, Janine came by to look at his latest artistic creations. She wasn't one bit pleased with what she saw. Embarrassed, Dev had to agree with her assessment. The inspiration was gone—it was as if his well of creativity had run dry.

Janine insisted that he not give up. She told him he had to keep working. She assured him all artists had dry spells, but they came out of them only if they kept working.

What Janine said made sense. It didn't matter how late he had discovered it; if he had talent, he'd always have talent. The decline in the quality of his work could have been a self-fulfilling profecy. He'd believed all along that if he got his strength back, he'd lose his ability to paint. However, the bottom line was that he didn't really care if he ever produced a satisfactory work of art again or not. At the moment he didn't have the drive he needed as an artist.

"Keep working, Dev," Janine said, hugging him for encouragement. "You must never give up." She added an encouraging kiss on the cheek to her farewell.

As Janine got in her car, Dev turned from her and noticed Carly was staring at him. When his gaze caught hers, he smiled and waved.

Carly returned his greeting without enthusiasm. She called Prints to her side and hastened into the house.

The door slammed at Mr. Cosgrove's house. Dev glanced behind him, then back toward Carly's home. For a moment, he considered following Cosgrove's example and going after Carly with a baseball bat. Maybe he could pound some sense into her, make her realize there was so much more to life than work.

But Cosgrove wasn't all caveman. He had a tender side too. Carly had told him the old man gave her flowers. That was the day Cosgrove had told Carly to take good care of her man, as though Dev and Carly had really belonged to each other.

Dev stuffed his hands in his pockets. He wanted Carly. He truly believed they did belong together, and, now that he was fully recovered, it was time he did something about it.

Dev dropped his arms to his sides and stalked into his house. He had nothing to lose. He walked directly to the kitchen, picked a number from the phone book, and ordered a bouquet of flowers to be delivered immediately to Miss Carly Ross, with a note inviting her to dinner on the day of her choosing.

Carly leaned against the door inside her house. Prints panted next to her, waiting for her to move. Tears rolled over her cheeks. She should have known better than to take the dog outside for some exercise while Janine's car was in Dev's driveway, but she'd told herself she was going to get on with her life. She wasn't going to let it bother her that Dev had chosen Janine.

A knife in the eye would have been less bother than the way her heart died whenever she saw Dev and Janine as cozy as any happy couple she'd ever seen.

Carly slid down the door and put her arm around Prints' neck. "How am I going to live and work next door to him, boy? I can't stand the heartbreak now. What will I do when they get married?"

Ever since Mr. Cosgrove had mistaken Carly and Dev for a couple, she'd wished with all her heart that what he said was true. He'd said Dev needed the love of a good woman.

Tears dripped down her cheeks. Dev did have the love of a good woman—Janine. Carly took a deep breath and wished with all her heart that it was her love that Dev wanted instead of Janine's. She'd give him every gram of her heart and share every day of her life if only he'd ask.

But he never would.

Carly decided she had no time for daydreams. Her work waited. She wiped her hands over her face, took a deep breath, rose to her feet, and marched to her work area.

Several unproductive hours later Carly gave up on work. She needed a break and a distraction.

It was a beautiful day. She decided to take Prints and go for a walk to Malena's house. She could use the company of her dear friend.

When Carly opened the door to leave, she found a young man standing on her stoop. He held a vase of flowers in one hand and was reaching up to knock with the other.

"These are for you." The tall, thin teenager handed her the flowers and left.

Carly watched the quick movements of the young man, then turned her attention to the fragrant flowers. The arrangement was a mixture of roses and carnations. She looked for a card, but there wasn't one. She set them on the counter and admired them as she smiled. "Mr. Cosgrove," she said, her heart warming at the thought of his perpetual romance with Mrs. Applebee. The roses were all white but for one single red rose, one almost like the arrangement the old gent had given her before.

She couldn't help but notice the significance of the single red rose, a symbol of love, among the white roses that signified the purity of Mr. Cosgrove's affection for Mrs. Applebee. "What a sweet beau that man was to Mrs. Applebee," she said out loud. "I wish I knew a man as romantic as the one who sent these flowers. His message is so clear it didn't even need a note." She fussed with the arrangement until it was perfect, then she and Prints went to Malena's.

Carly and Malena shared a heart-to-heart about anything that popped into their heads. That kind of talk always helped Carly see things more clearly. She had some changes to make in her life, and now she was ready to make them.

It was dark by the time Carly left Malena's. She walked back to her house thinking and solving problems along the way. When she reached her yard, she went to the maple tree that bordered her property line with Dev. She sat underneath it and stared at Dev's house.

Suddenly, he appeared in the window. Her heart leapt to her collarbone. Just the sight of him was enough to draw her to her feet. She reached for a branch overhead and took hold of it to steady herself.

Dev pulled the shade, and he was gone.

Carly looked up at the branch in her grasp. She remembered being under the tree with Dev early in the summer, him advancing toward her, her inching away from him.

She never should have backed away, but it was too late now.

She slithered down the trunk of the maple tree onto the ground and drew up her legs. She laid her head on her knees and cried for lost loves. Just like Mr. Cosgrove, she too lost the person she loved at five-zero-nine Valentine Lane.

Dev was in the kitchen getting a third cup of coffee when Prints bounded through the partially open back door. "Hey, boy," Dev said, putting his cup on the counter, "what are you doing running around this time of night? You're usually in your kennel by now." He picked up his coffee and took a gulp. "We won't bother Carly, fella. I sort of expected to hear from her after she got the flowers, but I guess I blew it again."

Prints bounded all around the kitchen, acting much

more excited than he usually did. Dev began to wonder if maybe something was wrong. "I'll tell you what, Prints, I'm going to take a look around Carly's house. You seem a little too restless to suit me. I want to be sure you don't have good reason for being so hyper."

Dev took hold of the dog's collar and walked him to the kennel. The feisty retriever didn't like being put away, and he let the neighborhood know it. Dev ignored Prints' apprehension and went about checking Carly's yard. The windows, the side yard, and the backyard all looked secure. The house was completely dark.

Carly must have gone to bed early and forgotten to take care of Prints. She did tend to be a little absent-minded sometimes in taking care of her dog.

Dev walked around to the front yard and checked the porch once more just to be safe. He didn't see any problem, so he headed home. As he passed the maple tree on the property line, he heard whimpering. His eyes shot to a figure leaning against the trunk of the tree. He looked closely in the moonlight. It was Carly.

With soft steps he got closer to her until he stood next to her. He bent down and touched the top of her head. "Carly? What's wrong?"

She yanked her forehead from her knees and pushed her gaze up to meet his. "Dev!" She scampered to her feet.

He stood when she did. "Are you all right?"

She wiped her cheeks and eyes with the sleeves of her coat. "I'm fine."

He brushed matted strands of hair from her damp face. He needed to know what had hurt her. Everything within him wanted to rectify whatever the trouble was. "You don't look fine," he said, smiling sardonically to hide his real concern. "Why don't you tell me what's wrong. Maybe I can help."

She stared up at him a long moment, her eyes glistening in the moonlight.

He raised his palm to her cheek and nearly drew her into his arms right then and there. She looked so vulnerable, so alone, all he wanted to do was comfort her and tell her how much he cared about her.

Carly blinked and more tears slid from her eyes.

Dev caught her other cheek with his remaining hand and wiped away her tears. "Tell me what's got you so upset."

Suddenly, Carly pushed at his wrists and tore his hands from her face. "I told you I'm fine." She shoved her hands into his chest and walked past him.

Dev's ire had never been so inflamed. If she didn't like him, fine, but she had no right to treat him like a mugger when all he wanted to do was help. He dogged her angry steps, tramping fiery paces of his own over fallen leaves and browning grass. His long strides easily overtook her shorter ones. When he reached Carly, he put his hand on her shoulder and spun her toward him.

She sent a piercing look up at him. Her long hair lay in thick masses around her face and shoulders. Her breaths plunged in and out.

He opened his mouth to scold her, but as he stared down at her dark enraged eyes his words stuck in his throat. The beat of his heart tripled, and he lost all control.

Dev pulled Carly into his arms as though he'd die that very second if he didn't.

The air from her lungs whooshed out of her as she hit his chest. Before she could take a breath to replace it, he covered her mouth with his.

His kiss was angry and passionate. His lips succinctly spilled everything within his heart. She'd hurt him with her rejection, and he had to get through to her how he felt, how much he needed and wanted her. If his flowers hadn't sent that message, maybe his physical contact would.

Carly struggled for a moment, and Dev kissed her even more thoroughly.

In eager response, she moved her hands to Dev's shoulders, over his biceps, down to his waist.

Dev gentled his kisses the instant she softened toward him. His hopes soared. At last she understood.

Carly pressed her hands into his back and ran them upwards along his spine. The fervor in her lips matched his.

Dev let go of her so he could take her face in his hands. He had to look at her. He desperately needed to see the intensity in her eyes. He pulled away from their kiss and looked down at her.

Carly clung to him with her lids down, gasping for breath, wavering on her feet. At last she opened her eyes and looked up at him.

She was so beautiful, he couldn't speak. Her eyes were as dark as coal, and she was intoxicated with passion.

She blinked and pulled her hands from his back. She wrapped her fingers around his wrists as he held her face. Suddenly, she closed her eyes and pushed his hands away. She stepped back, wiped her wrist over her mouth, and shook her head. "I've got to go."

He'd gone too far too fast. He reached for her and spun her back to him. "Carly, I'm sorry. I didn't mean to hurt you."

She glanced at his hand on her shoulder.

He released his grasp immediately.

Tears dripped from the corners of her eyes, and everything about her face went soft. With moonlight bathing her delicate features, her beauty intensified.

Dev ached to take her into his arms, but he didn't dare make a move toward her.

Carly wrung her hands, then clutched her throat. "I've got to go." She said the words, but she didn't move. Instead, she stared at him a very long time.

She suddenly lunged forward. As she threw her arms around his neck, she raised on tiptoes and kissed him with more care than Dev had ever known in his life.

His arms drew to her like magnets to steel. He wrapped her tightly inside his circle of strength and returned her sweet kiss.

Long moments of bliss began melting his heart like butter in the sun. Dev was certain he'd died and gone to heaven, and Carly was his everlasting life.

When she pulled away, Carly lifted her eyes to meet his. "Dev," she whispered, "I just wanted to say goodbye." She backed away from him. "I'm taking an office downtown." She took another step back. "I need to concentrate on my work full-time so I won't be seeing you or bothering you about noise or anything else anymore."

"But, Carly," he said, plunging toward her and taking her hand. "I don't understand."

She took a deep breath and folded her arms tightly in front of her. "What's to understand? You have your life, and I have mine. End of discussion." She spun around and walked away, then called over her shoulder. "Good-bye, Devin, and good luck with Janine."

She darted to the house as though a pride of lions were biting at her heels.

It took more strength to resist going after her in that moment than it had taken in a year to recover from his accident. He'd somehow ruined everything. He wasn't sure how. He was clueless as to why he couldn't make himself tell Carly how he felt about her. Whether it was his fear of another rejection or her consuming interest in her career that was the real barrier between them, Dev wasn't sure.

All he was certain of was that only one option remained for him. He'd call the union hall tomorrow and tell them he was coming back to work. Then he'd pack his things and return to Milwaukee. He didn't need the good luck with Janine Carly had wished him. His art career was over, and so were his chances with Carly.

For two days Carly agonized over her last encounter with Dev. She'd never been so torn apart by anything in her life. When he looked at her, held her, kissed her, she believed the message she saw in his eyes, felt in his arms, and tasted on his lips. He cared for her, possibly as deeply and hopelessly as she cared for him.

But he couldn't have feelings for her when he was involved with Janine. If he was the kind of man who'd toy with the affections of two women at once, she certainly wouldn't have anything to do with him.

The flowers from Mr. Cosgrove were the one bright spot in the last two days. The passionate red nestled among a sea of pure white, mixing to form a perfect pink—a love that was honest and ardent and totally devoted. Maybe some day she'd find that kind of love, but it would never be with Dev.

She inhaled the scent of carnations and roses deeply into her head and heart and wondered why Mrs. Applebee and Mr. Cosgrove had never gotten together.

A knock sounded at her door.

Carly flung the door open without looking to see who stood on her stoop.

"Good morning, sugar," Janine said, scratching a finger through her curls and winking. "I'm glad I caught you in. Dev tells me you're always working."

Carly didn't say anything. She merely stood in the doorway trying to close her gaping mouth.

Janine reached out and touched Carly's arm. "I won't keep you." She winked again. "I do have a big favor to ask, though."

Still not believing she was actually seeing Janine, she nodded her head.

"Good. I knew I could count on you." Again one lid fell, and another finger sought her scalp. "I'm having a little trouble with Dev, and I thought maybe you could help since the two of you are such good friends."

Carly felt her face ignite. Guilt jolted her gut.

"He's giving up on his art." She touched Carly's arm again. "He's always set store by your opinion." She squeezed her grip. "In fact, I don't think I could have ever enlisted him as a client in the beginning if

you hadn't told him how talented he was." She pulled
her hand back. She winked and scratched again. "Nat-
urally, we're way beyond awkward beginnings in our
relationship now, but he needs to hear from someone
besides me that he can't give up his art."

She tilted her head and sent Carly a coaxing grin.
"Can I count on you, Carly? Will you talk to Dev
about continuing his art? After all, if it weren't for
you, he'd have never started with me in the first
place."

Truer words had never crossed her ears. She still
could not believe Janine was standing in front of her,
much less that she was asking for her help with Dev.

"You'll do it, won't you?" Janine touched her arm
once more.

Carly had no idea why she was nodding. Then she
shocked herself by inviting Janine in for coffee.

Janine tightened her grip on Carly's arm, then
kissed her cheek. "Thanks a million for agreeing to
talk to Dev. I can't tell you how much I appreciate it."
She took her hand back, winked, and drove her finger
into her red curls again. "I'll have to take a rain check
on the coffee. We engaged girls have a million things
to do." She grabbed Carly's hand and shook it as she
sent one more wink her way. "If I don't see you before, I'll see you at the wedding next month." She took
her hand back and shook her fingers in the air. "A
Christmas wedding. Isn't that the most romantic thing
you ever heard?"

Carly watched Janine descend the stairs of her porch
before she closed the door. As she leaned into the
wood she felt the door open. She stepped back.

"Carly, sorry to bother you again, but I found this

out on the sidewalk. It looks like the kind of card they usually put with flowers." Janine said goodbye again and bounced over the porch and down the steps.

Carly looked at the tiny envelope in her hand. She stuffed it into the pocket of her jeans. She couldn't think of anything now but what Janine had asked her to do and what the art dealer had told her about her engagement. She and Dev were going to get married, and Carly had to go see Dev to discuss his art.

"Forget it!" Carly shouted to her empty kitchen. "I won't do it." She slammed an open cabinet shut. "And go to their wedding?" She opened the cabinet and slammed it shut again. "No way."

But she'd promised—not to go to the wedding, but to talk to Dev about continuing with his art. She always kept her promises. She vowed right then and there that she'd never make another promise again. Giving her word got her into too much trouble.

She took a deep breath. She stepped to the mirror in the foyer. She ran her fingers through her hair to neaten its disheveled appearance. She tucked in her light blue and yellow shirt and took another deep breath. "Might as well get this over with."

Carly carefully walked out the door. She watched her sneakers as she crossed the porch and stepped down to the sidewalk. She turned to her right and aimed herself toward Devin Serrano's house.

Now that it was all over between her and Dev, not that anything ever really started, she suddenly didn't mind seeing him again. His engagement to Janine must have taken place since their last encounter. He wouldn't have kissed her like he had if he'd been engaged then.

They were getting married next month. The man didn't believe in waiting.

She neared his house and began to focus on what she'd say to Dev. If Dev had given up his art, it really would be a shame. His work was beautiful. Though he wasn't the kind of man who was proud to make a living sitting down, he did have talent. It was practically criminal to waste it.

That's what she'd tell him. Throwing talent out the window was a crime.

She walked up the sidewalk to Dev's porch. She ascended the stairs and stepped lightly over his porch. She raised her fingers to his door and knocked. She didn't have to wait long.

"Carly!" Dev stepped back and opened the door wide. "Come in. I'm glad to see you."

She lifted her eyes to meet his. "You may not think that when I tell you what I've come to say."

Dev closed the door behind her. He leaned against it and folded his arms. "Oh?" he said, raising a brow and giving her a sardonic grin.

Carly backed up a few steps to put some space between them. She cleared her throat and stuck her thumbs into her back pockets. "Janine came by to see me a little while ago. She's worried about you. She said you've quit painting."

He moved away from the door and stood to his full height. "She had no business dragging you into this."

Carly shrugged, then flung her hair over her shoulders. "I guess she figured since I saw your work first, maybe I could have some influence on you."

He wiped a finger over his upper lip and lowered his eyes. When he looked at her again, he said, "I would say you have a great deal of influence on me."

Carly lifted her brows. "I do?" She cleared her throat again. "Dev," she said, her eyes pleading with him, "you can't quit painting. Your work is so beautiful. I can't understand how you could ever give it up."

"It's not so hard. Sometimes a man has to give things up, even things he loves." He reached out and touched her cheek gently. His eyes were full of pain.

"You don't have to lose what you love, Dev. Not if you really want it." Her heart broke for him and for her. He was hurting over losing his artistic inspiration, and she ached to have lost the only love she'd ever found.

Dev looked away from her. "You don't understand, Carly." He stepped toward the fireplace. He put his hands against the mantel and leaned into it.

Carly walked to him and placed her hand on his shoulder. "Why have you stopped painting, Dev?"

He glanced at her, then sent his gaze to the hearth below him. "I told you. Sometimes we have to give up what we love." He stood back and looked at her. "I'm going back to my job."

"In Milwaukee?"

He closed his eyes and nodded.

He was leaving. She was overwhelmed with a sense of both loss and relief. She wouldn't see him anymore, but she'd also not watch him start a new life with another woman.

Carly reached out and touched Dev's arm. "I can see why you and Janine want to live in Milwaukee instead of Pine Grove, especially since you're going back to iron work, but that doesn't mean you have to quit painting. You'll always be an artist. And there's another reason to keep painting, Dev," she said, squeezing her fingers around his arm. "Janine wants you to. A man ought to try to please his bride."

"What!" Dev's brows flew to his hairline. "My bride?"

Carly put out her hands in a calming gesture. "I'm sorry, was it still supposed to be a secret? Janine mentioned being engaged."

"And you think she and I—" Dev stopped in midsentence. He turned away from Carly and took a few steps before he spun back toward her. "When did Janine mention the engagement?"

"This morning when she came to ask me to talk to you about keeping up with your painting. But I've known a long time that the two of you were very close. I've seen the great affection you have for each other. You've been going out together for months."

Dev shook his head and stared at her in disbelief. "So you thought all along that Janine and I . . . and you assumed . . ." He drew in a deep breath and smiled. "That's why you didn't say anything about the flowers or the note."

"The flowers?" Carly shoved her brows together and stuck her hands into the front pockets of her jeans. Her right hand found the tiny card she'd stuffed there earlier. She pulled it out and looked at it, then at Dev.

"I see you've got the card with you." Dev stepped back to the fireplace and leaned his shoulder into the mantle.

"This card?" she repeated, wondering what he was talking about. What difference would it make to him that she had Mr. Cosgrove's card? Carly shook her head and closed her fingers around the little envelope. "We're getting off the subject. I'm suppose to be talking you into going back to painting."

Dev straightened and walked to her. "Yes, you are." He placed a finger under her chin and lifted her gaze to him. He stared a long moment into her eyes. "But before we get back to that topic, there's something you need to know."

He was too close. His presence, his scent, his touch conspired together to drain the strength from her knees. "What?" she said, her voice quivering. She hoped he answered before her legs liquified and left her melted in a pool on the floor.

"Janine is engaged, I'm not. She's marrying my attorney, Luca Atkins, next month."

Carly's legs regained every ounce of their strength, and she bounced back one giant step. Her eyes grew to the size of melons and her jaw hit her clavicle. "You mean you're not in love?"

"Not with Janine."

She stared at him tentatively. "With someone else, then?"

He closed his eyes and nodded, then he took three steps to the sofa. He reached behind it and pulled out a canvas. As he examined it carefully, his dark eyes softened and filled with affection. "With her," he said, turning the painting toward Carly.

As soon as she saw her portrait, her hand leapt to her throat. "But that's—" She lifted her eyes to his.

"Yes," he said, "it is." He leaned the painting against the coffee table and stepped toward her. "It's why I sent the flowers and the note."

"The note!" Carly pulled her right hand up in front

of her. "I haven't seen it yet. Janine found it on the sidewalk in front of my house. The flowers came without a card. I thought Mr. Cosgrove had sent them for Mrs. Applebee." As she was about to open the tiny envelope she looked up at him. "You sent the flowers?" One red rose among the white. Her heart raced. She dropped her eyes to the note and tore open the envelope. When she'd read the message, her eyes darted to his. "You sent the flowers? And you want to have dinner with me?"

He stepped closer and took her into his arms. "Not just one dinner, Carly, a billion and one dinners. And breakfasts and lunches and coffee breaks and picnics and everything in between. I love you, Carly. I've never loved anyone else."

She could hardly believe what he said. She inched her brows closer together. "You're sure?"

She felt a chuckle bubble up inside him as he held her closer. "Very sure." He stared down at her. "Don't you have something to say to me?"

She suddenly threw the note to the floor. Her arms flew to his neck. "I can't believe it," she said into his ear as she hugged the breath out of him. She pulled back from him and stared up into his dark eyes. She could feel her eyes moistening. "I've loved you for a long time, Dev. You don't know how it broke my heart to see you with Janine."

He leaned down and kissed her lightly. "From now on, Miss Carly Ross, you've got to speak up when something is bothering you—like all the noise that you complained about only once this summer and like what was going on between Janine and me. I want nothing but a completely honest and open and highly conversational relationship with the woman I hope to marry."

Carly's heart stopped in midbeat. "You want to marry me?"

He pulled back a little farther. "I know I'm going way out on a wobbly limb, but, yes, I do want to marry you."

"Honestly?"

He took a deep breath and squinted one eye shut. "Should I drop to my knees and propose?"

She smiled up at him, then pressed her cheek into his chest before she glanced upwards once more. "I'm not going to let you get far enough away to drop to your knees," she said, wrapping her arms around him for a good long hug. When she pulled back, she said, "I'll marry you, all right, and I know exactly what I'm going to give you for a wedding present."

"Hmm," he said, kissing her cheek and nuzzling her ear. "I can't wait to hear."

She pushed against him lightly until he moved back enough to look her in the eyes. "First I'll spend so much money on canvases and art supplies you won't have any choice but to paint."

He tightened his hold around her waist. "And then?"

She sent a flirtatious grin in his direction. "Then, mister woodworking toy man, I'm going to buy sound-proofing for your garage."

He lifted his hands to her face and brushed her complexion free of golden strands. Then he placed her face between his palms. "Now that's what I call being honest."

In the next second, as his lips sought hers, Carly reneged on the vow she'd made moments ago inside her house. She would make one more promise, and that one she'd keep for the rest of her life.